Cover Copy

One soul bound mate...one quest to find her.

Year 1211, Scottish Highlands.

As the Laird of Carron Castle, Coll MacKenzie has agreed to wed the daughter of his clan's allied chief in order to strengthen their bonds, only when he returns home after months away, it's to discover a woman ensconced within his household who could so easily shatter all his well devised plans. Fae-blooded Fiona is the only woman who's ever challenged him in ways that spoke to his very heart, and even though she holds the other half of his soul, he must still turn her away. His clan's future depends upon it.

Fiona has always been drawn to Coll's strength and courage, has always held the secret of his fae blood close to her heart, but now she's discovered they're soul bound, she has no intention of allowing him to turn her away. It's time to enforce the mated hunt, a chase all her fae kind long to begin.

Theirs is a battle of the very heart and soul, of desire flaring fierce and strong, and of a hunt across the beautiful wilds of Scotland during a time of war.

Books by Joanne Wadsworth

Books by Joanne Wadsworth

Regency Brides Series

The Duke's Bride, Book One
The Earl's Bride, Book Two
The Wartime Bride, Book Three
The Earl's Secret Bride, Book Four
The Prince's Bride, Book Five
Her Pirate Prince, Book Six

Princesses of Myth Series

Protector, Book One
Warrior, Book Two
Hunter (Short Story - Included in Warrior, Book Two)
Enchanter, Book Three
Healer, Book Four
Chaser, Book Five

Highlander's Touch

The Matheson Brothers, Book Nine

JOANNE WADSWORTH

The Fae Village

In the ninth century, the faerie king's youngest son visited a village along the shores of Loch Alsh and fell in love with the chief's daughter. The two wed and together created a half-blooded line born with the skills of the fae, a loyal line known as clan Matheson, a line guarded by the immortal fae princess, Cherub.

Fiona MacKenzie

The Chief of MacKenzie's stronghold, Loch Alsh, Scotland, December 1209.

Fiona walked alongside the shoreline toward a great cloud of dust pluming from her clan's warriors where they trained on the flat expanse of dirt near the stables. She searched amongst the hundred or so half-naked warriors wielding claymores as they fought in a battle of strength against one another. In the center of the training men, Coll, their chief's eldest son, swung his mighty two-handed sword and his opponent lunged forward and met his attack. Steel ricocheted loud against steel and Coll's biceps bulged as he held his position then heaved forward.

Such immense strength. His golden skin, all hot and sweaty, gleamed under the midday sun and the tight bands of corded muscle across his belly rippled with potent power. His kilt rode low on his hips and with each swing of his blade, the tartan whooshed above his knees and gave a mouthwatering glimpse of his toned thighs. Oh my. Her knees weakened and butterflies fluttered senselessly about in her belly, just as they always did when she caught sight of him in training.

"Did ye see that?" Next to the well, a serving maid nudged

the arm of another maid beside her, the two wenches ogling Coll so very openly.

"Och, he's a brawny one." The first maid giggled from behind her fingers. "He can flip my skirts whenever he so wishes."

Ugh. No more could she listen to those two floozies, and best she move on herself. Around the training yard, she strolled with her herb basket swinging in her hand. She had supplies to collect for their healer and with the skies clear and the wind fresh, there wasn't a more perfect day to venture out into the woods.

"This fight is done." Coll slashed and sent his opponent's sword flying.

Right at her.

Nay! She slammed to the ground, the gleaming blade whooshing over her head a mere hair's breadth away. Heart heaving and her fingers digging into the dirt, she gulped air.

"Fiona!" Coll bounded toward her, skidded in on his knees, dust scattering across her skirts. He patted her down, from her head to her shoulders then along her arms. With his hands on her hips, his fingers pinching in tight, he shook her. "What the hell were you doing walking so close to the training yard? You could have been hurt."

"I'm sorry." Shaking, terribly, she grasped his shoulders and tried to find her legs but got nowhere. "Please, help me up."

"I've got you." He stood in one fluid move, caught her hands and aided her to her feet.

"I'm still in one piece, and that's all that matters." She swayed, his broad chest smattered with dark hair so immensely close. "You—I—" She yanked her gaze up to his. "I mean, I should have been watching my step. I didnae mean to get so close to the fighting."

"Well, you did, and it'll never happen again. Am I understood?"

"Of course, understood."

"I mean it." Dark shadows circled his eyes, made all the darker by the fierce worry in his brown eyes.

"Are you no' getting enough rest again?"

"'Tis difficult to sleep under my father's roof when he angers me so. His fighting with clan Matheson must cease, but since there is naught I can do to change his mind at present, I've decided to leave for Carron Castle on the morrow rather than remain here for another week."

"You're leaving already?"

"My visit was only meant to be a short one. Carron is where I now call home."

"It's been three months since your last stay. Is Duncan leaving as well?" Duncan, his twin, held his own stronghold not far from Coll's along the shores of Loch Carron, and the two brothers were immensely tight. She searched the training yard and spied Duncan battling with his opponent. Although not identical, the two men were so close in looks that the odd man within their clan still mistook them. Never her. She'd always been able to tell the two apart.

"Aye, and Kyla too. She'll stay with me at Carron, and I've no doubt enjoy the respite from my father's heavy hand while she does. I intended on asking you to come as well. Kyla would enjoy your company."

"You truly wish for me to stay at your keep?" She'd love naught more than to travel with Kyla, one of her dearest friends and their chief's foster daughter. More than that, she longed to visit the stronghold Coll now called home.

"I more than wish it." A flicker of his need pulsed through to her, swirled around her empath senses, then just as quickly snapped off. Damn his natural fae-skilled barrier. It made it impossible for her to pick up his emotions when he threw it up.

"I wish I could come." Only now she couldn't, and how on earth did she explain Matthew to him, as well as her agreement to wed the man their clan called a gentle giant? It would be a shock for certain, as it had been for her when she and Matthew had spoken on the edge of the cliff this morn. They'd had such a heartfelt conversation, one in which they'd both recognized they could be the answer to each other's problems. She'd fallen in love with a man she could never have, and Matthew had lost the love of his life and needed someone to care for. He'd promised her he'd never insist on more than a friendship within their coming marriage, a most definite answer to her current prayers. She shook her head. "I'm sorry, but I—I'm no longer free to travel with you."

"So 'tis true?" His gaze darkened even further. "I caught word of a rumor about you and Matthew, but of course I ignored it. There isnae a chance you would ever agree to wed him."

"I can explain."

"You're saying the rumors are true?" Shock coursed across his face, pulled his brow down low and made white lines flare out from his eyes. "The warrior is twenty years your senior, and only recently widowed."

"There is more to it than that. Matthew's loss has taken a deadly toll on him and his pain is so strong. He also understands that my father is growing impatient in his demands that I wed. I cannae remain unattached as I am for much longer. Surely you see that." She glanced about. She'd definitely drawn the attention of the two wenches, something she couldn't allow. "Can we talk about this in private?" Coll deserved to hear all she had to say on the matter, because like Kyla, she'd been just as close to him and Duncan over the years and there was little she hadn't told him.

"Come with me." He caught her elbow, swept up her dropped basket and steered her farther away, around the stables and inside the back tack room.

Within the musty depths of the storeroom, only a trace of sunlight filtered through the cracks in the haphazardly placed wall planks. Reins and leads hung looped over spikes, while against the far wall, hay had been stacked four bales high and four wide.

Pacing before her, Coll gritted his teeth. "You've shown no interest in Matthew afore."

"He will always grieve for Elspeth. They loved each other dearly, and our marriage will be in name only. He has agreed to aid me, just as I've agreed to aid him." Elspeth had understood Matthew better than anyone in their clan could have since she'd been with him the day they'd both been captured by their enemy as children. Eight, Matthew had been at the time, and Elspeth seven when abducted by their enemy. Elspeth had unfortunately watched on as Matthew had been castrated against his will, then beaten and bruised to within an inch of his life. He'd suffered a great deal of injury, had struggled during his younger years to find his true place within their clan, but Elspeth had always known his very soul and the two, even though unable to consummate their marriage, had loved each other in every other way possible.

"He willnae touch me, even though we'll be wed. That is what I want, to be able to continue my work in healing others through my fae empath ability. Matthew shall be the first I shall heal. He needs a wife, and I also need a husband as you're well aware. I'd rather choose my own than have my father do so for me. With Matthew, I need never fear what is to come."

"You could offer him your healing without having to speak vows."

"I could, but that does no' take care of my unwed state." Breathing deep, she planted her hands on her hips. "We both know what's between us can never be explored, no' with you all but betrothed to Kyla."

"Kyla and I have to wed if we're to protect her Matheson kin from my father." Prowling closer, like a wolf on the hunt, he moved and she backed up fast, her back hitting the wall behind her.

"Stay back, Coll."

"It appears I have as little choice as you do in the matter of who I speak vows with."

"Sometimes life is unfair that way."

"You're damn right it is." Slowly, he narrowed his eyes, the turmoil within the deep hue of brown clear to see even though his emotions remained firmly in place behind his fae-skilled guards. "I dinnae wish to lose you to Matthew."

"Kyla is my dearest friend and I willnae see her lose her parents. She's protected them all these years and has no intention of stopping now. She might be your foster sister, your love for her never any deeper than that of a brother for his sister, but I love her, would never stand in the way of her need to protect her kin."

Colin MacKenzie had decreed that one day, one of his three sons would wed Kyla, and they all knew the son he'd choose would be his eldest. It was only a matter of time before their formal betrothal was announced.

"I hate it when you make sense." Gently, he cupped her cheek, stroked his fingers back and forth along her skin, the gold flecks rimming his brown eyes so soulfully captivating.

"You shouldnae be touching me like this."

"Aye, I should walk away." He swiped his thumb along her lower lip. "Yet every time I must ride away from my father's keep, my heart twists inside because I'm leaving you." Lowering his head, he touched his forehead to hers and whispered, "Do you remember that day under the waterfall?"

"I'll never forget it."

She and Coll, Kyla and Duncan, had gone swimming deep in the forest, the four of them taking an afternoon off together to visit one of their favorite places. She'd just come of age, and while the other two had been diving at the far end of the pool, she and Coll had left them behind and swum around the cascading water to the rocky ledge behind it. There in that serene, private place, they'd heaved up onto the ledge and seated on the edge, dangled their feet into the water. Sunlight had streamed through the clear sheet of water and sent beams of pale yellows, pinks, and blues dappling over them. She'd giggled as Coll had held his hand open, the beams playing across his palm, then she'd quieted, the moment so wonderfully sweet and surreal. Unable to help herself, she'd slid her fingers through his, looked deep into his eyes and fallen irretrievably in love. They'd sat like that for an hour, doing naught more than gazing into each other's eyes, until of course Duncan and Kyla had called out their names and they'd had to leave.

"This thing between us," she murmured. "This is why I need to accept Matthew's proposal. I dinnae wish to hurt Kyla, ever."

"Neither do I, and I've no idea how I'm going to make the change from seeing her as my foster sister, to seeing her as my wife, but I'll do whatever it takes to keep her and her true kin at the Matheson fae village safe."

"Which makes me so proud of you." Her heart clenched with how proud and hot tears burned behind her eyes. Nay, she wouldn't cry in front of Coll. He needed to see her strong, that she'd accepted her destiny wouldn't be with him, just as he'd accepted his wouldn't be with her. Sniffing, she pushed against his chest and forced him back a step. "Matthew intends on leaving here and sailing to Rhue Castle. Jeremiah has asked him to join his fighting force."

"Jeremiah is a thorn in my side, my younger brother a menace of the worst sort. You'll be as good as living under my enemy's roof at Rhue."

"Yet I'll still be safe there, and thankfully farther away from you." Once he'd wed Kyla, there wasn't a chance she wanted to remain close enough to see the two of them together.

"That's what you truly want?"

"For your sake, mine and Kyla's sake, aye."

"Come and meet me in the woods tonight, near the pool. You know the spot. I'll bring a hamper and build a fire." Tension tightened his muscles, his fists clenching at his sides.

"You wish to say a final farewell?" Eyes closed, she breathed deep, drew in his intoxicating scent, that of rich leather and warm skin and savored it to the depths of her soul.

"'Tis only right that we do." He stormed to the door, opened it and with one last glance over his shoulder muttered, "Dinnae be late."

Cherub –
The Fae Princess and Guardian to her Earthbound Kind

Carron Castle, held by Coll MacKenzie, April 1211, sixteen months later.

High on the battlements of Carron Castle, Cherub surveyed the rippling waters of Loch Carron as Kirk stood behind her, his nose buried against her neck and his teeth scraping back and forth across her sensitive skin. Cloaked and unseen to any other, she stretched her neck and grinned as her shifter mate nipped her flesh. "Are you hungry, my tempting bear?"

"Famished, and you always make a tasty meal." He slid his hands around her waist and drew her back against him, until every inch of their bodies touched and even more sparks flared. "How far away is Coll?" he whispered in her ear.

"He'll be here at midnight." The sun, a heavy orb of glowing orange, hovered low on the horizon as it began its descent. "Only a few more hours to go."

"He's been gone for so many months on his mission to the

far north of MacKenzie land."

"Aye, and missed a great deal with all that's happened here in his own keep during that time." The air swirled all around, lifted her white fur cloak and fluttered her regal blue gown about her legs. With her blond hair streaming back in the breeze, she lifted her arms and allowed the *air*—the element she controlled—to bring to her all the secrets it held. As her people's princess and an immortal time-walker, her duty remained with each and every one of her fae-blooded kind who walked this Earth. 'Twas her privilege to ensure the newly soul bound were brought together, no matter the divide of space or time that separated them, and this night, she intended on bringing Coll and Fiona back together again since their difficult parting sixteen long months ago.

The two of them had never truly understood that it had been a soul bond which had formed between them in their youth, right on that ledge under the waterfall, but soon they would. The proof would be undeniable, particularly now Coll no longer remained beholden to wed Kyla, not since his foster sister had been tracked down by her own soul bound mate and the two had wed. Aye, that had been one adventure she'd thoroughly enjoyed instigating, as well as seeing Ronan ensure the safety of Kyla's parents at the fae village.

"What has that sudden smile on your face, my elusive imp? I sense there's more you're not telling me." Her mate curved his big body around hers and she reveled in the moment.

"Circumstances were against Coll and Fiona from the very beginning."

"Aye, Coll always believed he would be the one to wed Kyla."

"Now Coll is going to be shocked to discover Fiona is no longer at Rhue Castle, but instead ensconced within his own household."

"He'll be more shocked to learn of how that's occurred."

He twirled her around by the shoulders. "When a man accepts his chosen one, there is no going back."

"My thoughts exactly, but our issue this time will be getting Coll to that point of acceptance. He may no longer be honor-bound to wed Kyla, but knowing he could never wed Fiona once he'd learnt of Kyla's marriage has sent him swiftly in the direction of another lass."

"Then we need to ensure he is sent just as swiftly back to the one his soul cries out for." One arm around her waist and the other her back, Kirk dipped her backward and touched his lips to hers. "Just as my soul cries out for yours and always shall."

"Are you trying to distract me while we're on duty?" She snuck her fingers underneath the hem of his white tunic and played with the ties of his black leather pants. "Because 'tis working rather well if you are."

"Mmm, distraction is good for the soul." He kissed her, his passion rising swiftly, just as swiftly as her own passion rose for him. "I love you, Cherub, never wish to live a day without you. I cannae even comprehend how Coll has survived this long without Fiona, or that he even allowed her to wed Matthew rather than to take her for himself in the very beginning."

"Coll's always done what duty demanded of him. He is his father's firstborn son and will one day be the Chief of Clan MacKenzie. Along with that position comes a great deal of responsibility."

Now though, 'twas time for Coll to balance those duties and to accept his mated bond now Fiona was once again free.

Which would mean she'd need to sprinkle a little bit of fae magic to make that happen.

A task she was more than up for.

Aye, let the next hunt begin.

Chapter 1

Midnight, a few hours later…

The welcoming yellow glow of the lit torches along the battlements of Carron Castle brought profound peace to Coll's soul as he rode the trail toward his stronghold in the dark of night, his men galloping behind him. So many months he'd been gone, but now he'd returned from his mission to gather more warriors to his and Duncan's cause with an additional two hundred men at his flank. Slowly but surely, he and his twin brother had made inroads into distancing themselves from their heavy-handed father and soon they'd successfully strengthen their two strongholds as they both desired.

"Our laird returns!" The call came from the head guardsman standing at attention next to the two-story gatehouse. It echoed toward him across the night-shrouded waters and brought a wide grin to his face.

Up high on the ramparts, standing guard at the corner crenellation, Duncan raised one leather gauntleted hand. Spurring his horse on, he galloped along the high rocky cliff overlooking the inner channel of Loch Carron, kicking up dust in a cloud that swirled all about.

Under the high arch, he rode, then jerked on the reins and slowed his war horse. He brought the heavily-snorting beast to a halt in the center of the bailey and steered his mount in a circle as he breathed in the renewed sight of his home.

The leather of his saddle creaked and his chain mail swayed as he swung a leg over.

He dismounted and landed on the gravelly inner yard with a crunch, his feet once again upon his own treasured soil. Being home again soothed his very heart and soul, as it hadn't been soothed in so incredibly long. Sixteen months long. Not that he'd been away from Carron for all that time, but for some reason his return this night seemed all the more peaceful. Strange. That emotion only ever assailed him when Fiona was near, that and dire need as well.

"'Tis about time you returned home." Duncan marched down the barbican's stone stairs, the hilt of his sword strapped to his back gleaming in the golden glow of the moon, his black hair shining a midnight blue on the ends and a recent gash slashing his muscled forearm where his shirtsleeves had been rolled to his elbow. This was his brother, his twin, the one man who'd always understood him as no one else ever could.

"Beyond time, and it appears you've been in the wars." Still grinning, he tossed the reins of his horse to a stable lad who dashed forward to take them and clasped his brother's forearms in a firm warrior's hold. "I've missed you, brother." Searching Duncan's intense gaze, he sought the knowledge he needed, an unspoken sense of knowing which had always existed between them. The responding twinkle in his twin's eyes exhilarated him. "You love her?"

"She's a fae compeller from the Matheson village, a woman who's not only my mate, but also holds the heart of a warrior. I honestly didnae expect to find her as I did, and Ella certainly led me on a merry chase across the Western Isles in pursuit of her, but now I've captured her and made her mine."

"When shall I meet her?" He'd received his brother's missive about the news that he'd wed while visiting one of their allied clans, that of the MacRaes.

"She's at Ardan House and expecting me to return on the morrow. Come with me when I leave in the morn. We'll ride together."

"I wouldnae miss the chance of meeting Ella Matheson."

"MacKenzie now. She's taken my name."

"Of course, my apologies. Have you had any further issues with the Chief of MacDonald since your marriage took place?"

"The MacDonald has no' attacked again since I wrote to you."

"Good, and Kyla?" He'd been struck almost senseless after reading of both Duncan's marriage to Ella, then on the next page, Kyla's marriage to Ronan Matheson as well. So much he'd missed, yet never again.

"Her mate has well and truly claimed her. Ronan is in fact our birthmother's nephew, is now well aware of the secret of our fae blood. He holds the battle skill as you and I do, is a warrior of immense strength and has proven himself most worthy of her. Ronan also spoke to her parents in the village and all there are taking every precaution in case of a strike by our father. All has turned out rather well on that front. The fae shall live." Words spoken quietly, their cause to ensure the fae lived one they kept a secret from all but their most trusted, and even though he trusted his men implicitly, as well as the chiefs of their allied clans, they still took all care.

"Then Ronan is worthy indeed. Have you received any word from Father?" He'd be furious upon hearing of Kyla's marriage to a man who wasn't one of his sons.

"Furious, as is to be expected, although I've also sent him word of my marriage to Ella and that seems to have appeased him a touch. She's a fae compeller, her skill so very strong, no' that I married her for any reason other than I love her. These are difficult days though, and I'm deathly sick of Father's demands. 'Tis a shame we cannae break away from him completely."

"Agreed, but one day he shall no longer walk upon this Earth, and we must bide our time until then." Already they'd done a great deal to separate themselves, and when his father breathed his last, he needed to be able to take control of their entire clan, including his father's holding should he wish to continue his mission of ensuring the fae lived. For now, he remained here at his own stronghold, while Duncan maintained his own keep a mere hour or two's ride away.

"Coll MacKenzie!" Hands on her hips, Kyla glared from the top step, moonbeams streaming down from high above and bathing her in a stunning shimmer of gold, from her hair to her gown and slippered toes. She appeared the angel she'd always been, even with the furious frown on her face. "'Tis about time you returned home."

"Come here and beat me up if you wish."

"You can be certain I will." Although she'd never been able to stay angry at him for long, and it appeared she couldn't this night either. With a catch to her breath, she grinned and dashed toward him, her vibrant skirts swishing and golden-red locks streaming behind her as she ran.

"Slow down."

She jumped and he barely opened his arms in time to catch her. Twirling her around, he couldn't help but laugh as she did. Her joyful giggles echoed about the bailey, his own deep chuckles almost smothering hers. Hell, he'd always loved her, as a brother loved his sister, their foster-relationship forever strong.

"You've been gone for so long. Six months, you brute." She peppered his cheeks with kisses. "You should have sent a scout ahead with a message you'd be arriving this night. We were no' expecting you for another day, and I also almost tripped down the stairs in my hurry to get to you. I've missed you so much."

"So much that you went and wed another man, when I'd

dearly hoped it would be me."

"Liar." She thumped his chest. "You're as glad as I am that we'll never have to speak vows."

"True." He hugged her tight. "Where is your husband? I wish to meet Ronan Matheson and thank him profusely for taking you off my hands."

"Then you'd best put her down afore you do." A warrior stood at the front door wearing black battle leathers and his claymore strapped to his side, a man who could almost pass for him with how close in looks they appeared. Aye, they were clearly related by blood.

"Welcome to the family, Ronan." Gently, he set Kyla down and extended his hand to Ronan as he strode toward him.

"I've been awaiting this day as much as Kyla has. 'Tis good to finally meet you." Ronan shook his hand and stared at him. "Well, 'tis no wonder Kyla first mistook me for you."

"Glad I am to finally meet you too, and for keeping such a watchful eye on Kyla. She can be quite the handful at times."

"Excuse me, but I'm standing right here." Kyla slapped him in the chest again. "I want to beat you up so bad."

"You can do so inside if you wish. Come, let's all speak further in my solar, to ensure our coming conversation isnae overheard. I have much to tell you all." He walked across the yard, leaving the whickering of the horses behind. Aye, he needed to inform them of the agreement he'd recently made with the Chief of MacRae, one which involved him soon speaking marriage vows with the man's eldest daughter, Elizabeth.

He stepped into the great hall, pulled off his riding gloves and stuffed them in his pocket. Hefty barks echoed and two big dogs raced past the roaring fireplace. They skidded across the polished floorboards, their ears alert and drool flying as they bounded toward him. He prepared himself as only he could for Beast and Buster's welcome home. Lowering to one knee, he prayed he'd survive the coming impact.

They hurtled into him and he fell back, got smothered in hearty licks and giant paws thumping his chest. Now this he'd surely missed. He hauled his dogs closer and reveled in the moment of finally being home again amongst his nearest and dearest, his pets included.

"They've missed you almost as much as the rest of us have." Kyla knelt next to him and gave both the dogs a good tummy rub as they rolled all over him. "Do you recall the day Fiona first discovered these two?"

"I'll never forget that day." Five years ago, in one darkened corner of the stables at Loch Alsh, he'd found Fiona sitting with these two pups as they'd tried to nuzzle at their dead mother's belly. Their death had been all but close as well, only the empath in Fiona had arisen and she'd scooped the newborn critters up, taken them to her chamber and over the weeks ahead had nursed them until they'd grown strong enough to lap milk from a dish and chew meat on their own.

"They'll live, Coll. They're really going to live." Fiona has gushed to him one night in the quietness of her chamber, right next to the warmth of the crackling fire as he'd visited her to check on the pups.

He'd eased down on the thick woolen rug beside her, touched his palm to her cheeks all rosy and red, her excitement brimming forth as she'd played with the two little critters. *" 'Tis your dedicated touch alone which has seen them live."*

"They know they're going to survive as well. I can sense their emotions." She'd wriggled closer to him, popped a kiss on his cheek.

"What was that for?"

A blush. *"Um, for helping me with them when needed."*

"Mayhap we should name them now you're certain they're going to survive."

"Aye, they should have names. You choose one and I'll choose the other. You go first." She'd handed the eldest of the

two puppies to him, one pure black in color while the other, still pure black, held a tip of white on his tail to mark the two apart.

Lifting the eldest pup up, he'd touched his nose to the pup's nose and got a sloppy lick across his chin in thanks. *"This one shall be named Beast, 'cause he's a beast of a licker."*

"That's a good, strong name for a dog." Jiggling, she'd lifted her own pup with its white-tipped tail flicking from side to side, higher. *"I'm calling this one Buster."* She'd grinned at him, so damn adoringly, her smile near melting his heart.

"Beast and Buster." He'd wanted to kiss her cheek right back, and had barely restrained.

"They'll be our dogs."

"Aye, always ours."

"Coll?" Kyla squeezed his shoulder and stirred him from his memories. "Do you still wish to speak this night? If you need to catch up with Beast and Buster some more, then we can speak to you in the morn."

"Nay, my apologies. I just got lost in my thoughts." With one last hearty rub down each of the dog's backs, he rose to his feet then strode down the side passageway toward his solar. He pushed open his door and a maid scrambled to her feet from in front of the blazing fire.

The lass stuffed one loose lock of her brown hair back under her frilly cap and wiped her hands against her aproned skirts. "Your fire is lit, my laird." She bobbed her head. "Would ye care for a tray and a tankard of ale?"

"Aye, a tray sounds fine, but make it whiskey instead of ale." He and his men had ridden hard this day to make it back to Carron by midnight. His hunger and thirst beat at him.

"As you wish." The maid bustled out.

Moonlight slanted through his window overlooking the inner courtyard and filtered over the top of his chunky wooden desk and the pile of seneschal's accounts gracing one side. He pulled out his desk chair and sat while Duncan eased into one of the two corner padded chairs and Ronan took the other before tugging Kyla onto his lap. His new cousin and now brother-by-marriage, stroked one hand over the slight rise of Kyla's belly. Well, well, it appeared she was with child, which no one had yet mentioned to him.

"Congratulations," he murmured, motioning to her bump.

"We thought no' to include this news in the missive Duncan sent you. I wanted to tell you myself of the babe." With her flushed cheeks, Kyla was so adorable.

"I'm glad you waited to inform me." He tapped the desktop, rapping away.

"You look more worried than glad right now."

Elbows to his knees, Duncan eyed him from his seat. "Spill whatever it is you've no' yet told us."

"You're aware I was with the Chief of MacRae when I received your missive, yet what I have no' told you yet is that after learning of Kyla's marriage, I entered into a discussion about forming a possible marriage of alliance with John MacRae." He leaned back, breathed deep. "I'm to wed his daughter, Elizabeth. She and her father are due to arrive here afore the end of the week, at which time we'll speak vows."

"Is there a reason for your sudden rush to wed, other than to secure our alliance?" Duncan scrubbed a hand along his jaw, looking far more worried than he should. "I didnae expect this news from you on your return."

"I understand 'tis sudden." Although he'd had good reason for wishing to wed quickly. The shimmering image of his fiery empath flared to vibrant life within his mind, as it always did when his thoughts turned to her. With her mass of red curls tumbling to her waist and her blue eyes, so soulful and beautiful, focused only on him, he drowned in the exquisite beauty of his Fiona, the woman who'd forever remain beyond his reach.

"Coll?" Kyla frowned at him. "Where did you just go again?"

"Old memories is all." He smiled at her, tried to ease a little of her worry by doing so. He might no longer be honor-bound to wed Kyla, but now he was honor-bound to wed Elizabeth, the contract he'd entered into almost as binding as any marriage contract could be. It had been the only way to ensure he didn't ride hell bent for Rhue and steal Fiona away from Matthew. Dishonor her or the gentle giant of a man she'd wed, he'd never do. Flicking his gaze between Kyla and Duncan, he muttered, "Neither of you can tell me it isnae a wise move to wed Elizabeth. Forging a stronger alliance with clan MacRae is imperative."

Duncan shuffled forward an inch, his sword hilt bobbing in its baldric. "The MacRae's eldest son now possesses a large parcel of land near us, and of course wed a fae-blooded Matheson lass a few years past. A marriage of alliance isnae entirely necessary considering the familial fae-blooded ties we now hold with them. You can change your mind if you wish. John MacRae would understand."

"Nay, I've already signed an agreement and even spoken binding betrothal vows before her clan. All that remains left is for the formal ceremony with a clergyman."

"What's Elizabeth like?" Kyla leaned her head against Ronan's shoulder.

"She's been well trained to manage a keep."

"You dinnae wish to marry for love? What if you too discover you hold a soul bond with a woman of fae blood, just as I have discovered I do with Ronan, and Duncan has discovered his bond with Ella?"

"There is no such bond for me." And never would be. "Elizabeth shall be your new sister come the week's end."

A knock sounded.

"Enter," he called out.

The maid returned and set a tray on his desk, one holding a steaming bowl of stew and a corked flagon of whiskey. "Is there aught more you need, my laird?"

"Aye, I wish to bathe after I've eaten. See to a tub being filled in my chamber, then inform me once 'tis done."

"Of course." She closed the door behind her as she bustled out.

"What else can you share about her?" Another probing question from Kyla.

"Elizabeth has red hair and freckles." He scooped the slice of crusty bread wedged to the side, dipped it into his stew and took a hearty bite.

"I meant in how well the two of you get along." Brow arched, Kyla dipped a finger under the white lace edging of her velvet bodice and freed a gold necklace. A disk dangled from it, one holding an engraved word on one side and as she twirled it about, the firelight reflected another word etched on the reverse.

"What does that say?" He gestured to her charm.

"It says Kyla"—she flipped it over—"and Christina." She turned her attention on her mate, sank one hand into his hair and grinned all silly at him. "Christina being the name Ronan had first known me by at the fae village afore my capture by Colin MacKenzie. 'Tis my true name." She turned her smile back on him. "No' that I dinnae love being called Kyla. Oh, and, Coll, you've missed meeting my parents. They joined us here for a short while and have only recently returned to the village. I wish you could have met them."

"I'll meet them when they return for another visit. I hope you told them they're always welcome here."

"Absolutely."

Aye, never would he turn one of Kyla's kin away, not when they were his blood kin too. Stretching his chainmail-clad legs under the table, he crossed them at the ankle, uncorked the whiskey and tipped the flagon to his lips.

Duncan wandered to the window and gripped the ledge, his gaze ever-watchful on the courtyard beyond where torches mounted on the stone walls spread their warm glow across the stony ground and up across the battlements and their patrolling guardsmen. Turning back, Duncan rested his backside on the sill, his dark hair a few inches longer than usual and almost brushing his shoulders. "You should know that I extended the barracks at Ardan House and can now house some of these additional men you've returned with."

"Then feel free to take half of the men who arrived with me back to Ardan. We'll spread our additional numbers out so we can ensure we hold the length of Loch Carron with ease."

"Will do."

Another knock and Meg returned and dipped her head at him. "Your bath awaits you, my laird. I'll aid you with your chainmail if you wish."

"That would be greatly appreciated." He heaved to his feet, his chainmail heavy after the long hours he'd spent in it. Ridding himself of it without his squire's aid wouldn't be easy, and since he had no intention of finding the lad when the maid could see to the chore, he gladly accepted her aid. Clapping Duncan and Ronan on the back, as well as dropping a kiss on the top of Kyla's head, he said, "I'll see you all in the morn. Sleep well."

"You too." Kyla blew him a kiss. "'Tis wonderful to have you home."

"'Tis wonderful to be home." A home he'd soon be welcoming his new bride into.

With a slightly heavy step, he walked out of his solar and up the stairwell, the maid following quietly behind. On the third floor, he opened his chamber door and entered. His large bed dominated the space with its magnificently carved posts that rose to the ceiling, the royal blue canopy sweeping down each of the four sides and secured at the corners with golden ties. His desk sat in the corner, the piece a replica of the one in his solar downstairs.

Gently, he trailed one finger along the desk's polished

surface, the rolls of parchment he'd left there on his departure still sitting between his stoppered ink well and his personal journal covered in red leather, the pages within an accumulation of memories he'd added to over the years, although not these past six months he'd been away.

He picked up the precious journal with its lock on one side, the key always stored in his trunk. Cait, his father's wife and the only woman he'd ever known as his mother, had gifted him with this journal on his seventh birthday, mere days before she'd taken a chest illness and passed away. He'd loved her, no matter she hadn't been his true birthmother. She'd raised him and Duncan with all the love she could have offered, and this gift was one he'd forever cherish. Aye, that day she'd gifted him this journal, she'd told him to store all his memories within and he'd never missed a life-altering moment.

In it, he'd included the night when he and Duncan had first met Kyla. Their father had called them down to his solar and as they'd stood before him, Colin MacKenzie had lowered to his haunches, his gaze narrowed and his next words shocking them. He'd told them that the mother they'd always known until the day she'd passed, hadn't been their mother at all. Before he'd wed Cait, the Chief of MacLennan's daughter, he'd in fact handfasted with a fae lass named Beth Matheson, a lass who'd unfortunately passed away while birthing them both. The knowledge of who their true mother had been had remained a secret from even them until that day. Even now they told so very few, only those they implicitly trusted.

Aye, never did their father wish to lose the lands and dowry he'd gained with his marriage to the MacLennan's daughter, and that could still happen should the truth become fully known to one and all.

Behind him, the maid tossed another log on the fire, her cheeks flushed and the neckline of her kirtle somehow far lower than when they'd entered. She crossed to him and hunkered down, her frilly cap slipping off her head and her long brown locks cascading down to her waist.

"The water awaits ye, my laird." With a tug, she removed his boots and set them aside then stood and loosened the ties of his chausses. She wriggled them down past his braies, her gaze flicking over him as she scooped up her lost cap and stuffed it in her apron pocket. With care, she lifted one of his arms out of the heavy sleeve of metal, slid the protective mail over his head then down his other arm and with a *clunk*, set it on the chair next to the tub filled with steamy hot water. "You're a kind and caring laird, fair and never harsh," she murmured.

He breathed deep. "Thank you, lass."

"Ye must get mighty lonely when ye are gone for so long from home."

"What age are you, Meg?"

"Eight and ten, sir." She walked to the side table and picked up the bar of soap. "Do ye wish for me to scrub ye as ye bathe?"

She wouldn't be the first maid to make the offer and he doubted the last, but never had he accepted any of them. Hands on the hem of his under-tunic, he pulled it over his head, tossed it into the corner wicker basket and opened the door. "I've no need for aid, will manage well enough. Thank you for your kind offer though."

"Are ye certain?" She dunked the soap into the tub and built a lather between her hands, then with the bubbles smeared between her fingers, walked around to his back and rubbed. "Ye cannae get your back cleaned once I'm gone. At least allow me to scrub ye clean here."

With a long sigh, he stood still as she smoothed over his skin, her touch tender-light.

"Ye have a mighty lot of muscle." The maid stepped around him, her hands gliding over his shoulders then his chest as she worked the bubbles across his skin.

"May I ask something of you, Meg?"

"Aye, I'd like that." Eagerness shone in her eyes, her hands sliding down his sides and over his hips, the thin brown linen of his braies knotted at his waist thankfully protecting him from her roaming hands dipping any lower. "Would you pour me a drink afore you leave? I find I'm still thirsty."

"Oh." Chin lowered, she glanced at the flask of wine on the side table then stepped away and wiped her hands on her aproned skirts. Flask in hand, she poured the wine into a silver goblet and handed it to him. "Ye must be most weary after such a long journey. Rest well, my laird."

He would only ever long for one woman's hands on him, and it would never be this maid's or even his future bride's. Unfortunately, he'd lost the chance to wed the only lass he'd ever—well, no use going back over that yet again. Fiona was in the past and that's where she needed to stay. His future was now set, and it was with Elizabeth MacRae.

He closed the door after the maid, shucked his braies and stepped into the bath and sank down. Warm water flowed over his back and chest and once he'd dunked fully down and wet his head, he came back up and worked the soap through his hair then went under again and rinsed.

With his head resting on the lip and the fire's flames flickering bright, he closed his eyes and allowed Fiona's sweet image to once again flicker back to vibrant life within his mind, just as he'd allowed it to do for each of the long months he'd been away. He just couldn't help himself. Self-punishment and all.

Not long after he'd left here six months ago, he'd even visited her at Rhue Castle for a few days, and while there of course taken great care not to be alone with her. He'd only made the journey to Jeremiah's keep to ensure he spoke to a few of his men he kept there as spies and receive updates since Jeremiah could be as devious as their father could. He'd also made certain the men he'd recruited knew to keep an eye on her, that they guarded her well, and of that he'd needed to ensure, no matter they'd fully and completely parted ways.

With her image still strong in his mind, he gripped his hardening shaft and with a firm hand, pumped himself and allowed more images of his fiery empath to consume him.

She was the woman he'd always wanted.

And the woman he could never have.

* * * *

A man's low growl then deep groan stirred Fiona to wakefulness. Water splashed somewhere close by. She elbowed up in bed and searched her darkened chamber. Her fire had died away some hours ago although the odd ember still glowed and for some reason, so too did a sliver of golden-red light shimmering through from under the connecting door between hers and Coll's bedchamber. How odd. He wasn't due back until late tomorrow, and she'd certainly be awake when he did.

Another groan, and distinctly Coll's deep rumble. Goodness. He was back.

Covers shoved away, she hopped across the cold floorboards in her nightrail and gripped the doorknob. Another moan. Mayhap he'd been hurt during his mission which was why he'd returned earlier than expected. She needed to check on him.

She opened the door with nary a noise, snuck inside and tiptoed around his bed. A fire glowed in the hearth and flames flickered high. A wooden tub sat before the fire and Coll rested in the bubbles facing away from her, his head on the lip. Water dripped from the wet ends of his midnight-black hair and splashed the floor.

He moaned again and she barely breathed.

Water sloshed and spilled over the side, his hand below the bubbles moving frantically back and forth. Nay, he wasn't hurt but bringing forth his own pleasure. She'd caught sight of the odd warrior doing so in a darkened corner of the keep when no others were around and knew what was about

Usually, she backed quietly away when such happened and left them to their privacy, only her feet wouldn't move. Aye, she was done leaving Coll, or allowing him to leave her and she'd missed him terribly, had been longing for his return since Duncan had aided her in her escape from Rhue following Matthew's death some months ago. This was the moment she'd been waiting for, to confront Coll and demand he no longer set her aside.

"Fiona." He mumbled her name, gritted out, "I need you."

She needed him too, desperately, just as she always had.

A flare of heat spiked in her core, his demanding words making her nipples bead and poke into her shift. Never had her body come alive except when near him, and this night was no exception. So too he was no longer honor-bound to wed Kyla, and as the fates would now have it, neither was she bound to Matthew. This was her only chance to grab the future she desired, which would only ever be with him.

"Dinnae leave me." He grunted some more, his shoulders shaking as he shuddered, then his hand fell limp to his side in the water.

"I give you my word I'll never do so again, Coll." Inserting her steadfast resolve, she stepped clear of her hiding place behind the royal blue bed-curtains and clasped her hands before her. "Welcome home."

"What the hell!" Water flew as he jerked around. Wide-eyed, he stared at her. "You cannae be real."

"I'm so sorry to have interrupted your bath." She jabbed her curled toes into the floorboards. "But you called my name and I've decided I'm never going to turn away from you again."

"Nay, you truly cannae be here. I must be dreaming." He rose from the tub, water glistening on his broad chest and coursing in rivulets down his abs. The drops caught in the dark thatch of hair at his groin, right where the long length of his cock swayed between his legs, the head plump and thick and—oh my, she couldn't take her gaze from his manhood. He stepped closer, his muscular legs long and strong and his cock which had softened after he'd sought his pleasure, once again jerking upright. He halted in front of her, fisted his hand around his shaft and stared into her eyes. "A dream more real than any I've ever had about you afore."

"If you're dreaming, then so am I." She may still be an innocent, but she'd also grown up amongst warriors aplenty. Men who'd caroused from time to time and got a little bawdy. One certainly couldn't live within the walls of a castle with hundreds of men about and not stumble upon the odd coupling as they sought their pleasure with the wenches.

She'd just never seen Coll so stripped down and very naked before.

Back a step, she inched until she hit her back on the corner bedpost. She cast her gaze down his impressively built body once more, his muscles all sleek and hard and—she cleared her throat. "So, I see you're a big man, ah, everywhere."

"Aye, I'm most definitely dreaming, because that is exactly what I would have wanted you to say when you first looked upon me." The gold flecks flickered brighter in his stunning brown eyes and with one finger crooked, he motioned for her to come back to him. "Dinnae be afraid of me, my fiery empath."

"I've never been afraid of you, but then I've never quite seen you like this afore." Return she would though. She inched forward, until the tips of her toes touched the tips of his bare toes, then she tipped her chin up and looked him in the eyes. "You appeared to be enjoying your bath, while you spoke my name."

"Aye, I always speak of you when I bathe and dream like this." He released his cock, wrapped his hands around her waist, dipped her back off her feet and touched his mouth to hers. He kissed her, so whisper-soft, as if he wished to savor the taste of her then with a low growl, he deepened their kiss, his tongue sliding over hers in a kiss that completely scattered all her thoughts.

Naught had ever felt so right.

Coll was kissing her, for the first time, and he was completely naked too.

"I want to touch you," he breathed into her mouth.

She nodded, so lost for the aye she needed to speak.

"You're the perfect illusion of my sweet Fiona." He set her back on her feet, tugged the tie at the neckline of her nightrail then loosened the laces all the way to her navel. Slowly, he parted the fabric and exposed her breasts. "Och, what a sight to behold."

"You like what you see?" She certainly liked the way he looked, but then she always had.

"I do." He gave the folds of her shift still clinging to her hips a tug and the cotton slithered down to her feet and pooled on the ground.

She should have been embarrassed, but the emotion just wouldn't rise around him. She wanted this, him touching her and her touching him.

"I want to devour every inch of you."

"By all means, go right ahead." She had no intention of halting him now, not when she'd been waiting a lifetime for this moment. She wanted him to make her his in every possible way.

"Make my dreams soar, Fiona." He scooped her up, dropped her on top of his bed's brown fur covers then slid in over top of her and brought their flesh together without even a single inch separating them. "Touch me, just as I'm touching you."

Oh, sweet heaven. This moment had now moved far beyond her wildest dreams.

Touch him, she would. She grasped his shoulders, stroked down his muscled arms then around to his back before dipping lower, right over his firm buttocks. This was exactly how she'd always wished to touch him, and now she'd started, she had no intention of stopping.

It was time to claim the man she'd always wished to claim.

No more would she allow another to stand in their way.

He was hers, just as she'd always been his.

37

Chapter 2

This moment was what Coll had wished for his entire life and he intended on bedding his dream Fiona until neither of them could breathe for the pleasure. This magical hallucination of her would have to keep him satisfied for all the years to come once he'd spoken his marriage vows with the MacRae's daughter. "Tell me you want this," he whispered against her lips.

"I want this."

"As do I." He caught one of her silky red locks tumbling across his covers and twined the long length around his finger. Her breathing hitched and he seized her mouth and saturated himself in the taste of her, in the only woman who'd ever consumed his every thought, both day and night.

"You kiss so divinely." She clasped his shoulders, her nails digging in like a claiming then she rubbed her body against his, the friction of her soft skin against his hairier body so sublime.

Damn, he'd never be able to hold on for long if she kept tormenting him in such a way. His cock throbbed, so achy and full even though he'd just brought himself to a peak in the tub.

Dreamily, he slid one hand along her hip then down into the V of her groin and cupped her mound. Silky red curls, the same rich and vibrant shade as her head, guarded her entrance. Heat pulsed there and gently, he slid one finger along her nether lips as he lowered his head to her lush breasts.

The rosy tips begged to be sucked on and he dived in, wrapped his mouth around one hard nub and as her legs quivered against his, her soft moans urging him on, he took her nipple deeper into his mouth and sucked, hard.

She cried out and he nearly did too, this moment one he'd forever cherish, never wished to awaken from, this woman forever in his heart and always in his dreams. Hell, of course she'd wed Matthew, and he'd committed himself to Elizabeth, but this moment was made in the heavenly realm of his fantasies and he intended to let no one else intrude upon it.

He popped her nipple free of his mouth, lifted up and captured her lips. He wanted to drink her in, to slide his tongue into the moist recesses of her mouth and taste her very essence. Inhaling her white rose scent, one that had haunted him these past sixteen months, he consumed her with one passionate kiss after another.

He got drunk on her, and she melted into him, one hand roaming down his side and over his hot shaft. She wrapped her fingers around him, made him whimper and turned his body into a blaze of roaring heat. Pulling back an inch so he didn't come right then and there, he flicked her ear with his tongue and rumbled, "I want to taste every inch of you, for you to shatter against my mouth. Does the thought of that frighten you in any way?"

"Shattering sounds splendid." A sultry haze darkened her eyes. "I love how you speak to me."

"There are so many things I want to do to you, and for you to do to me."

"Tell me."

"I want you to take me in your mouth and stroke me with your tongue, to have you sitting on top of me and riding me hard. I want to pulse deep inside you and never let you go." He'd never spoken to her like this in his life, but in his dreams he could. She was everything to him and always had been, and his cock was weeping for more. Hard as a hammer, he wanted to take her to the edge of reason right along with him, and he fully intended to.

"With Kyla now wed we can be together as one." She glided one finger over the tip of his erection, so damn teasingly.

"Grip me proper."

"Those are three words I want to hear you say every night for the rest of our lives." She swirled over the head, stroked down his length right to the base and softly cupped his balls. "Promise me you will."

"Woman," he growled and jerked in her hold. "You are a wicked temptress." He eased down her body, intent on making this dream-filled night count. Scraping his cheek across the soft skin of the upper swells of her breasts, he rumbled his pleasure.

More. He had to have more, and aching for another taste of her sweet nipples, he circled the pointed tips with his tongue, first one and then the other, and as he did, she sank her fingers into his hair. He devoured her, from her breasts to the flat plane of her belly and down each of her legs until he laid between them and nuzzled her inner thighs.

Heat rushed forth and a sweet honeyed scent encapsulated him. She was so incredibly wet. With one finger sliding into her womanhood, he delved deep, his blood rushing through his body and making him twice as hard in mere seconds. Damn, if he wasn't careful, he'd come before she did, and that he couldn't allow, not even within this dream.

"Oooh, so close." She dropped her head back, her eyes closing and back arching.

"I'm beyond close." He pushed her legs farther apart, his senses burning into a frenzy of need. She was like an elixir of the most decadent sort, tantalizing and teasing him beyond his endurance.

Aye, no more could he wait.

He caressed the wicked heat of her passage, fondled her deep and allowed his hunger for her to roar forth and consume him. He wanted one taste below, intended on stroking her there with his tongue, only she wriggled down and gripped his cock.

With an incredibly possessive touch, she rolled her thumb over the head of his shaft, which made the fiery burn sizzling at the base of his spine ricochet around and blaze to the tip of his dick.

Pre-come oozed forth, his cock weeping for more and she pumped him, just as he'd done with himself in the tub. His cock filled and lengthened further. Hell, no more. He couldn't take any more.

With his blood roaring, he drove two fingers into her and touched a spot that had her crying out his name and shuddering against him. Her inner muscles clamped down on his fingers and dragged them ever deeper inside her, right where he wanted his cock. Only too late. She was coming and so was he. His essence spurted free in one long and hot rush between her fingers and he roared his pleasure before slumping onto his side next to her.

Everything darkened, his dream disappearing so swiftly as exhaustion took him.

* * * *

Fiona struggled to draw in a breath as she floated somewhere far beyond her body. When she'd worked Coll's cock in long pulls and he'd thrust his fingers inside her, 'twas as if he'd finally staked his claim on her and such an array of emotions had flared so strongly through her. Giddy pleasure. Heart and soul fulfillment. A rightness than ran bone-deep. Everything she'd ever desired with him had been granted in this one single moment in time.

Slowly, she drifted, his light snore keeping her safely cocooned in her dreams. All she'd ever wanted was him, for him to claim her and even though he hadn't taken her maidenhead, he most definitely had made love to—

A cock crowed and she jerked awake.

Light streamed into his bedchamber and she squinted against the bright glare.

Making love with him had clearly knocked her out for hours. Him too by the looks.

He moved not an inch, dark bristles shadowing his jaw, and one sheet pulled up over his lower body and hers, the fur covers all askew.

The portcullis rose from within the stone-arched entrance gate, the clunky sound of its chains reverberating across the bailey. A new day had dawned and since dark shadows still ringed Coll's eyes, 'twould be best if she left him to his sleep and didn't awaken him. He had arrived back so late last eve, and must have ridden hard all day to do so.

They could speak when he fully awoke.

Carefully, she shuffled off his soft mattress, tucked the covers over him then scooped up her nightrail puddled on the floor. Smiling, she folded and set it on the end of his bed. It would be a reminder of what they'd done, which she hoped he didn't still consider a dream when he awoke since he'd seemed so adamant about that while they'd loved each other.

Limbs loose and her body completely satisfied in a way she'd never experienced before, she crept out of his bedchamber and closed their connecting door with a quiet snick.

In behind her dressing screen propped in the corner, she scooped up her clothes which she'd laid there last eve on the three-legged stool.

Clean shift in hand, she eased it over her head then donned her favorite red velvet gown, which swished over her hips and whooshed to her ankles in a soft fluttery fall. White embroidered detailing lay stitched into the low neckline and along the ends of the long sleeves that draped over the backs of her hands. She'd always adored this gown and reverently, she picked up the matching white embroidered girdle and belted it at her waist before adjusting the long tasseled ends at the center where they swept down to her knees.

She stroked the soft velvet, just as she'd done when she'd first spied this fabric at the markets from amongst several bolts of cloth. Coll had accompanied her to the village that day and then watched her avidly as she'd admired the dressmaker's fine wares. Sadly, she'd had to leave the bolt of cloth behind since her father would never concede to her spending yet more coin on fabrics when things were tight.

A fortnight later though, Coll had knocked on her door one morn and stood there with a silly grin on his face. In both hands, he held a sizeable package wrapped in brown cloth and spoke words she'd never forget. "*I couldnae resist purchasing this for you.*"

"*What is it?*" Over the years he'd often gifted her small trinkets, from tiny carvings he'd whittled from wood, to silk hair ribbons he'd purchased at the markets, as well as the odd treat from the village baker which he'd brought home. This though was clearly no trinket by the size of it.

"*I couldnae help myself.*"

"*Clearly that is so.*" But she'd given in quickly, so excited to see what he'd brought her and naught could have surprised her more when she'd peeled back the brown cloth and exposed the red velvet she'd adored at the markets. She unfolded the fine fabric, the layers falling to her ankles. Nay, not just velvet, but velvet now sewn into an exquisite gown. He must have asked the castle's seamstress to do this. She hugged the gown to her chest then hugged him, squishing the fabric between them. "*I cannae believe you did this for me.*"

"*Will you accept my gift?*"

"*Of course.*"

"*Thank you.*" And just as quickly as he'd come, he'd strode off down the hallway with a jaunty whistle and disappeared downstairs.

Never had a man given her such a treasured gift, and she'd worn the gown he'd gifted her with that day, just as she did this new day. He would understand the meaning behind it when he saw her, or at least he'd better understand it.

Sashaying out from behind the screen, she walked across to her side table. Gently, she ran a brush through her hair and left her locks lying loose and long down her back, then donned her riding boots and tucked her eating dagger into its wrist sheath under the sleeve of her gown.

Out the door, she fairly skipped, then bounced down the stairs. Such a heady mix of joy filled her, made her want to sing and shout, and to declare to all the world that the man she'd adored for so very long had now returned and finally claimed her. No more did he belong to another. He belonged to her, just as she'd always belonged to him.

Into the great hall with its massive wooden-beamed rafters rising to an imposing height overhead, she pranced. Sunshine streamed in through the tall windows and sprinkled golden and bright over the wooden floorboards. Across the far side of the hall, serving maids bustled about as they brought out jugs of warm cider, fresh bread and platters of boiled eggs and laid the food upon the tables. The hall remained fairly empty, but not for long. Soon it would be filled to the brim with warriors aplenty.

Next to the blazing fireplace, Beast and Buster sat with their tails slapping the hearth, eagerness sparkling in their eyes as they awaited her. Coll had taken them with him at her request before he'd left her that last day at his father's keep. She'd never be permitted to take them to Rhue and they'd always been as much his dogs as they'd been hers. Now, she hurried across, hunkered down and wrapped her arms around their big heads and got a hearty lick on each cheek when she did. "Did you see your master has returned?"

Beast yapped and Buster thumped his white-tipped tail

harder.

"I'm excited too." She scratched under their chins and Beast rolled onto his back before raising his paws. Buster followed suit and with both bellies presented to her, she giggled and gave them both a hearty tummy rub.

"Fiona, there you are." Beaming, Kyla whisked across, her forest-green gown swishing about her legs and the waist draping over the delicate roundness of her belly. "Coll rode in a few hours ago, has returned far earlier than we envisioned. I'd wished to plan a banquet in celebration of his return for this eve, but Coll intends on riding to Ardan to meet Ella first. We'll have to delay the feast until tomorrow's eve. Do you wish to aid me in the preparations?"

"Of course." She'd love to, and Coll would most definitely wish to meet Ella, his new sister-by-marriage. The lass was a fae-blooded compeller with a hypnotically sweet voice that could see a man move to do her biding without him even being aware of it. A very sought after fae skill, and also a very rare one, although she always took great care when using it. "I'm aware Coll returned earlier than expected. I awoke when I heard him bathing in his chamber afore bed last eve." She hugged Kyla, beyond excited to share her news. "I have something of great import I need to tell you, and afore this hall fills."

"Then come. We'll speak while we break our fast. My babe grows restless and kicks up a storm this morn. Hungry, I'm certain. I most definitely am." Kyla grasped her hand and tugged her up onto the dais. Her friend waved out to one of the maids walking across with a tray of steaming oats and a platter of crusty bread and the maid set bowls for them both down at the high table, bread as well, then hustled over to finish setting out the other tables.

"Where's Ronan?" She pulled out a seat for Kyla. "I wish only to tell you of my news for now." Privacy was needed, particularly since she'd never whispered a word to Kyla of her feelings for Coll, not when doing so would have hurt her.

"Ronan has already eaten and ridden out to see to the security on our eastern border, so whatever you have to say can remain just between us." Kyla eased into her seat, lifted the milk jug and added a splash of milk to both their bowls.

"Wonderful, because 'tis of a very sensitive nature." She perched next to Kyla, dunked her spoon into her oats and ate a mouthful. Warmth raced to her empty belly and she grinned anew.

"Oooh, please hurry up and tell me your news of great import." Kyla poked her in the arm. "You can barely sit still and you have such a glow to your cheeks."

Jiggling even more and no longer able to hold back a moment longer, she whispered in a rush so no others could overhear. "I didnae just awaken at hearing Coll's return, but also opened the connecting door between our rooms and, ah, spoke to him."

"Well, dinnae stop there. You spoke of what?" She picked up a slice of crusty bread, dunked one end in the small bowl of honey and bit into it.

"Of his dreams."

"And those would be?"

"Of touching me."

"Pardon?" Kyla coughed and thumped her chest. "Did you just say Coll has dreamed of touching you? And exactly where did he wish to touch you?"

"Everywhere, and we did touch, everywhere." She shoved a slice of bread into her own mouth, her cheeks so hot.

"You and Coll? Oh my." Kyla nabbed her tankard of apple cider and slugged it back, her gaze darting from her to her drink and her again.

"I know this will come as a surprise, particularly when I've never told you of my feelings for him, but of course I couldnae afore this time. You two were as good as betrothed throughout most of your childhood."

"I dinnae know what to say. I mean, you two have always been rather close, but never close in the way of, well, touching as you've said."

"I wish I could have told you sooner. I'm sorry."

"Dinnae apologize to—wait." She shook her head. "What of Coll's betrothal to the Chief of MacRae's daughter? He's set to wed Elizabeth MacRae by the week's end. He told Duncan and Ronan and I all about it last eve. Did he speak to you about it as well?"

"Pardon?" Her head spun and her belly rolled. Surely Kyla jested. "He never mentioned any betrothal."

Kyla gripped her hand. "Coll has no knowledge that you're staying here, or likely any knowledge of what's happened to Matthew since he's been nowhere near Rhue Castle in a very long time, and Duncan and I certainly never wrote of it in the missive we sent to him. He's invited the MacRae and his daughter to join him here so they might speak their vows. An agreement has been signed and they're set to wed." Kyla squeezed her fingers tighter, her eyes swimming with tears. "How deep do your feelings for Coll run exactly? Tell me everything."

"I've always loved him, to the depths of my heart and soul." Without question she had and still did. Hot tears burned behind her own eyes. How could he agree to wed another woman, and then touch her the way he'd done last eve? Unless he truly had believed her presence there was naught but a dream. Damn it all. He must have.

"I can see you're in shock." Kyla pulled her in close and hugged her. "Now that I'm aware of your feelings for him, and of the depth they run, have you ever considered that mayhap a soul bond is at play? It might have gone unnoticed by you both until now considering his duty to me. 'Tis entirely possible."

"Soul bond or not, he's now betrothed to Elizabeth MacRae

and I should never have expected him to remain unattached for long after learning of your marriage. He is the firstborn son of a great chief, will one day lead our clan and be expected to make a very profitable match. Elizabeth is the daughter of a chief and I'm naught more than the daughter of a warrior under his father's command. What have I done?"

"Nay, I willnae hear you worry about what you've done, no' when 'twas done in love." Kyla scraped her chair closer and muttered under her breath, "First, you must discover if there is in fact a soul bond between you, because if there is you cannae allow him to speak vows with another woman. He'll regret doing so, until the end of his days."

"And how exactly do I work on discovering if there's a bond?"

"You need to make him stake his claim by beginning the hunt."

"*The* hunt?" She was well aware of what the mated hunt had been like for Kyla when Ronan had begun it with her only a few months ago. Duncan too had been forced on the hunt for Ella when she'd attempted to evade him. "I dinnae wish to evade him, but speak our issues out face to face."

"That you cannae do when he's clearly gone and gotten himself betrothed to another woman. Nay, when Ronan hunted me down, he never gave up on his pursuit until he'd captured me. So too, you must instigate the hunt with Coll and see if he makes chase. You'll know the moment when the intricate strands of the mated bond begin taking form between you. It's undeniable. You'll be driven toward him, and he'll be driven toward you, and since he's now touched you as you've said, well, that'll only make his chase of you even more intense."

"He allowed me to wed Matthew." Aye, he'd never set chase after her back then, had in fact allowed her to escape him by leaving her first, although of course the circumstances surrounding that time in their lives had been difficult considering his and Kyla's soon to be wedded state.

"Aye, but will he allow you to escape him a second time once he learns you're now free to wed him? I'm certainly no longer standing in your way, and that is the question you need to have answered. He most certainly does no' love his bride-to-be. All Coll wishes to do in marrying her is to ensure our allied bond with clan MacRae is strengthened." Kyla rose to her feet and motioned toward the stairwell. "Go and pack a bag and leave as quickly as you can. 'Tis time for the hunt to begin, and you need to extend your wings and fly, to force him into acknowledging the bond if it does in fact exist between you."

"You're right." She certainly wasn't ready to let Coll go after all they'd shared last night. If a bond existed between them, then she was about to find out. She nodded at Kyla. "The hunt shall begin this very day."

* * * *

Stretching in bed, Coll stirred from the incredible dream he'd saturated himself in during the night and cranked one eye open. Sunshine streamed through the window and he blinked against the vivid brightness and groaned. In no way was he ready for this new day.

He heaved the fur covers over his head and eyes closed, brought the vivid and dreamy image of Fiona—completely naked and lying underneath him—back to glorious life. When he'd bounded from his bath last eve, he'd found her in his chamber with clear desire flaring in her eyes. He'd walked across to her, tipped her back and claimed their first kiss and hell, it had been an incredible kiss. Her mouth had softened under his then as he'd deepened his possession, she'd returned his passion and naught could have pleased him more.

His illusion of her had been intense. She'd allowed him to strip her nightrail from her, to slide her into his bed and permit his touch. He'd sucked on her glorious nipples, stroked over her creamy flesh and even dipped his fingers inside her hot channel, and while he'd touched her, she'd trailed one finger over the head of his cock and made his balls clench so damn tight. His shaft had swelled to a throbbing peak and then she'd smiled, like a vixen, and he'd gotten completely lost. Together they'd come, soaring right into the heavens and for the first time in his life he'd finally felt complete, as if she was right where she belonged, with him and only him. A dream of course, which it always would be considering he'd walked away from her sixteen months ago.

He'd allowed her to wed another man, and now he was set to wed another woman.

A woman who'd be here before the end of the week, which meant he needed to get moving. His clansmen would be awaiting him and he had much to do this day, including a visit to Ardan House so he might meet his new sister-by-marriage. A smile returned to his lips. He certainly had no intention of keeping Duncan from his chosen one for any longer than necessary.

He pushed the covers away and sent something white fluttering off the end of his bed. Scooping it up, he went ramrod straight. Was this a woman's nightrail?

Strange. That hadn't been—wait—surely his encounter with—nay, his time with Fiona had surely been a dream. Aye, he'd been exhausted after almost an entire day riding in the saddle, but even so he'd never mistake the real Fiona for the illusion he'd created. He eyed the connecting door between his chamber and the next one.

Nightrail in hand, he strode to it, hauled the door open and marched inside. Sunshine beamed in through the open window and shimmered across the thick burgundy bedcovers gracing the bed. Next to the corner dressing screen, a side table held a dish of bright hair ribbons and an ivory brush and comb. He snagged the brush and plucked a long strand of red hair from within its bristles. That shaft of hair definitely belonged to a woman, and ironically it was same long length as Fiona's. Twining the length around one finger, he strode to the ambry and flung the burgundy curtain wide. The interior rail held a score of gowns, all neatly pressed in an array of deep colors, from forest-green to midnight blue and rich red. Fiona's favorite colors, ones which always brought out the rosiness in her cheeks and made a stunning contrast against her pale skin.

Ah hell. There had to be an answer for this.

He lifted the soft cotton of the nightrail to his nose and breathed in the delicate scent of white roses. How had he missed that? 'Twas definitely Fiona's scent, only if she was here, then why on earth was she here? And where was Matthew? He hadn't noticed the man about the keep when he'd arrived last eve.

Damn. If she hadn't been an illusion and he'd actually touched her, while she was wed to another man, then Matthew had every right to slice his head from his shoulders, no matter their marriage was in name only. That made no difference. She was a taken woman.

He tossed Fiona's shift onto her bed since it was clearly hers and stormed back to this own room. From his trunk, he pulled out a clean pair of pants in a faded brown leather, donned them and a loose-sleeved white tunic. Feet stuffed into his leather boots, he belted his sword at his side and stalked to his side table.

Splashing water from the jug into the basin, he muttered several unrepeatable words. What a right royal mess he'd now gotten himself into. Soap in hand, he built up a lather and slapped the suds on his jaw, gripped his dirk and scraped the stubble from his jaw.

"Coll?" A knock rattled the door. "'Tis Duncan. We need to speak."

"Come in." Aye, they most definitely needed to speak. Why hadn't his brother warned him of Fiona and Matthew's arrival?

Duncan strode in and shut the door, his padded cotun slung over one shoulder and his blue trews fastened at his waist and black tunic open at the deep V. "We need to speak about Fiona."

"You're damn right we do." Another scrape of his blade, his anger at himself flaring higher. "I noticed she holds the connecting chamber to mine. Why is she here? And why the hell didnae you mention her arrival to me last eve?"

"There wasnae time."

"You should have made time." He splashed the remaining suds from his jaw and dabbed his chin dry with a cloth. Tossing it in the corner wicker basket, he snapped at his brother, "Tell me everything."

"Kyla, Ronan, and I brought Fiona back here safely from Rhue Castle, no' long afore the Twelfth Night and Yule celebrations began. She's been here for months." Duncan leaned his backside against the windowsill, the long length of the inner channel of Loch Carron weaving into the forested distance beyond the window.

"What of Matthew? Did you no' bring him here too?"

"I have bad news about Matthew." Duncan scrubbed a hand through his hair. "I hate to tell you this, but unfortunately Matthew suffered a nick during a training session some months ago, the smallest arm wound, but it festered and he took a fever. He passed away."

"What? But Matthew was hearty and hale the last time I saw him at Rhue." He'd also left implicit instructions with the three men he kept within Jeremiah's stronghold that should anything happen to Fiona, to send word to him immediately. This constituted sending word.

"I can assure you Matthew has perished." Duncan pushed off the windowsill and gripped his shoulder. "If you'd known of his passing, I've no doubt you would've returned for her. I did what you would have done and brought her here where she'd be safe."

"Safe?" Such shock rocked through him, his breath coming harder. "What did Jeremiah do to her?" Of all their clansmen, his younger half-brother had been the only one over the years who'd ever made her feel unsafe. He could get rough with the lasses when not watched, although he'd set Jeremiah straight a time or two about remaining well clear of Fiona. "If he touched her in any way, I'll kill him."

"'Tis a long story, but suffice to say, Jeremiah forced Ronan and I to sail there after causing mayhem here at Carron, then after learning of Matthew's passing while at Rhue, we brought her back with us. She feared for her life, Coll. I couldnae leave her there a day longer, no' when Jeremiah wished to make her his leman." Duncan growled under his breath. "She worried greatly that even should she say nay to him, he'd soon force her to his will. Knowing Jeremiah as I do, I didn't doubt his intentions would be dishonorable. Kyla is so happy to have her near us again, and so am I. The four of us have always been so close, and Ella adores Fiona too. Being that we all hold fae blood, there is no better place for her than once again amongst us."

"She would be safest at Ardan House with you rather than here within my own walls." He was to wed another woman, and if Fiona remained widowed and within his arm's reach, he'd want to keep touching her. That he couldn't do. He had his future wife to consider, as well as his entire clan. Gritting his teeth, he muttered, "Is she aware of my upcoming marriage?"

"She is now. On my way to see you, I spoke to Kyla below-stairs and she informed me she'd spoken to Fiona about your upcoming nuptials."

"How did she take the news?" His heart clenched in on itself. Never would he have wished for Fiona to hear of his impending marriage vows from anyone other than him.

"I didnae see her, thought it best I come and speak to you first."

"I need to find Fiona now." He nabbed his black coat from the ambry and rushed out the door. He'd speak to her, right this second.

"You seem so anxious." Duncan followed him as he jogged down the passageway and took the stairs two at a time. "Why is that?"

"I'll explain soon." He entered the great hall where a good hundred of his men sat in chattering groups at the trestle tables as they ate the midday meal. He'd missed a great portion of the day, had never arisen so late, but then he'd never been so exhausted. At the dais, Kyla set her goblet down and waved out.

He stalked across to her, planted his hands on the table before her and tried to keep his voice even. "Duncan has informed me that Fiona is here and now resides with us."

"Aye, but she and I spoke this morn and now she's gone."

"Gone?" He lost one very necessary heartbeat.

"She returns to her father on Loch Alsh."

"What?" He lost a second and thumped his chest, his heartbeat pulsing right out of time.

"She took the news of your betrothal hard and wished to leave. There is naught I could do to stop her." Kyla settled one hand on his arm. "She told me about what happened between the two of you last eve. That you touched each other."

"You and Fiona touched?" Duncan stared at him with wide eyes and mouth agape. "Why did you no' tell me?"

"I would have soon." He heaved his gaze back to Kyla. "Which guardsman did she take with her?"

"I'm unsure if she took a guardsman, only that she rides as far as the village beyond Ardan House, then hoped to cross the mountains on foot. She intended on asking the village stable master to have your animal returned to you as soon as possible." Kyla's gaze softened. "Do you sense the need to chase her? Because if you do, you should ride out as well."

All he sensed was painfully deep anger, and mostly directed at himself. She'd left him, never given him the chance to explain his actions. She must hate him for what he'd done by touching her so freely. He certainly hated himself.

"Do you, Coll?" Kyla stared at him. "Wish to chase her that is?"

"Provided she's taken a guard, there's no need for me to follow her to her father's home." His future was here, with a lass named Elizabeth MacRae, not with the woman he'd given up sixteen months ago. Only, everything within him recoiled at that thought.

* * * *

With her black cloak flapping back from her shoulders and red velvet skirts plastered to her legs, Fiona bent low over her horse's back as she rode the high cliff side trail between Carron Castle and Ardan House. The forest rose high on her right, the towering pine trees swaying in the brisk breeze, while to her left the cliff fell sharply away and the churning waters of the loch crashed hard into the black rock wall and misted high.

The hunt had begun, and now 'twas time to see if a bond had formed between her and Coll.

She certainly wanted him to stake his claim and come after her.

With her mare's reins firm in hand, she slapped her knees harder into the animal's flanks and quickened her already fast pace. She jumped jutting tree roots and ducked under the odd low branch, the satchel she'd packed with some necessities bumping about on her back. Pine needles scraped her arm, and the cool wind nipped at her nose.

She rode on, until she finally neared Ardan House, although before she could be seen by Duncan's guardsmen on duty, she brought her horse to a halt at the top of the winding trail that veered steeply downward toward his stronghold. Below, the castle sat at the edge of a secluded bay along the loch, its gray fortified walls rising high with a two-story gatehouse built to the right of the main arched gates. This keep stood as strong and secure as Carron Castle did, while two days' ride to the south,

Colin MacKenzie's stronghold sat at the gateway to their MacKenzie land on Loch Alsh. There, she'd find her father, not that she wished to find him. Nay, she wished for Coll to catch up with her first.

Although no stopping for now. She had to make certain the hunt would be good.

She turned away and urged her horse onward along the wooded trail toward the village where she'd be able to safely leave Coll's horse with the stable master to have the animal returned to him. One could cross the mountainous plateau by horse, but 'twas best done on foot considering the sheer ruggedness of the land.

Determination spurred her on and she hugged her horse's neck as she rode.

Chapter 3

Coll stormed through the bailey and out the postern gate, such unease rolling through him. Over a hundred of his men already trained along the shoreline near the meadow leading to the forest, dust swirling into the air as they battled, their swords clanging and fierce grunts ricocheting toward him.

"I take it we're riding out as well?" Duncan questioned from beside him.

"Nay, I simply need to check she took a guardsman with her."

"So, you've touched her, hmm?" A glint of intense interest flickered in his brother's eyes.

"What of it?"

"When I first sensed the mated bond forming between Ella and I, she enforced the hunt in her determination to ensure I saw the truth about our bond taking form. You and I never had the benefit of living within the Matheson fae village, never saw firsthand how deep and all-consuming the bond could be."

"What are you trying to say?" The wind whisked his hair about his neck, the soft touch as gentle as Fiona's fingers had been on his skin last eve.

"You've never been able to abide the touch of another

woman, just as I never have."

"Again, your point is?"

"When two are mated, 'tis their touch alone and no other's which we can allow. Might I ask if you enjoyed touching Fiona last eve?"

"I allowed her to wed Matthew, simply rode away knowing it would happen. That isnae something any man would do with his chosen one. Even I'm aware of that." Nay, no bond existed between them, and of that he was certain. Up ahead, a lanky-legged lad in loosely belted pants brushed down a sleek brown war horse before the stables, while another lad saddled a destrier for the guardsman awaiting his mount. The warrior thanked the lad with a nod, mounted his steed and galloped into the forest.

"I was so wary at first of giving Ella my trust," Duncan continued as they walked, "of allowing her to learn exactly who I was and that I held fae blood, but she knew we were soul bound and within a short time I couldnae deny that bond either. What if Fiona is your mate?"

"I must seal my alliance with the MacRae. 'Tis my duty to ensure our clan survives and thrives." Scrubbing a hand over his nape, his fear for Fiona rose stronger and pulsed through him. No matter Duncan had worked hard to keep their land clear of their enemy while he'd been away, they could still slink in and he'd allowed Fiona to escape him and never should have. She better damn well have taken a guard. Surely none of his men here would have allowed her to leave without first ensuring one of them rode out with her.

"I can see the fear in your eyes." Duncan squeezed his shoulder. "We'll find her and you'll make things right."

"The only right thing is for me to remain here." He stepped up to the stable lad and muttered, "Mistress Fiona rode out this morn. Which guard did she take with her?"

"None, my laird. She took the trail between here and Ardan and knows the way well. 'Tis safe."

"She rides farther than Ardan this day."

"She didnae say so." Fear rippled within the lad's eyes. "Are ye certain?"

"Very, and in the future"—he gritted his teeth—"you'll never allow her to leave without first ensuring she has a guard with her, no matter where she rides to. Saddle my destrier and my brother's as well. Be quick about it, lad. We need to leave with all haste."

"Aye, right away." The lad whistled out to another boy and the two scurried inside the stables.

Impatient, Coll paced the cliff top. He wouldn't consider the danger she'd now put herself in, because if he did, he'd surely lose it. A seagull soared overhead, circled then dove into the tumbling waters of the loch. It squawked as it heaved back out of the rolling surf with a fish flapping from its beak. Another seagull gave chase and the first landed on the rocks, guarding its catch and hissing at the second bird wishing to steal its plunder. That was how he felt right now, as if he needed to catch and guard his plunder. He shook his head of the unhelpful thought.

"Two horses saddled, my laird." The lad returned, reins in hand.

He thanked him, checked the cinch, slung his war coat on and bounded into his saddle.

Beside him, Duncan mounted up, his leather saddle creaking.

"Let's be off." No more could he wait. He thrust his knees into his horse and galloped out of the yard, dust swirling into the air.

'Twas time to hunt Fiona down and ensure she never made the mistake again of leaving his keep without first taking an adequate guard. He'd certainly never admit to himself there might be another reason why he needed to make this chase. Aye, she'd undertaken a dangerous journey alone and with her being close kin, she came under his protection. He wouldn't fail her now.

If only he hadn't touched her last eve.

Aye, he'd always wanted more with her, to the depths of his very soul, although that didn't mean a mated bond had formed between them. He would never have allowed her to wed Matthew if that were the case.

"You appear worried. You can speak to me about anything, brother." Duncan eyed him from low in his saddle as the wind swept through the trees and rustled the pine branches.

"Fiona and I have always been close, more so than I've probably ever let on." The words tumbled forth and he cleared his throat. "That's no' to say we're mated, because we arenae."

"What if you're wrong?"

"I'm not."

"These past few months, she's been awaiting your return as keenly as Kyla and I have."

"That does no' mean we're mated."

"Every time one of our warriors has sought her company out, she's politely turned them away." His brother raised a brow. "She's a widow, Coll, could so easily take her pick of any of the men here should she wish one of them for her husband. They all adore her, always have and always will, but now that I'm aware of how you've touched her, so much more makes sense. You've always struggled to keep your gaze off her. When she entered a room, you watched."

"I believed my time with her last eve to be merely a dream. I didnae know I was actually touching her in truth."

"Of course you did." Duncan snorted under his breath. "You're just ignoring your base instincts, that of a man intent on binding his chosen one to him. It'll all become clear sooner or later."

"I agree I've always been infatuated with her, but that is all." A lie. He'd been far more than infatuated with her over the years. From that day he'd swum with her in the pool around to the ledge behind the waterfall, he'd sensed something tugging at his very heart. That hour they'd sat with their fingers interlocked had been the most precious hour of his life. Naught had ever felt so right than to have her sitting next to him, not that he'd ever admit that to Duncan right now when it would only feed his brother's insistence that they were in fact mated.

"If she is your mate then the bond between you will surely deepen now you've spent such an intimate time together. Trust me. From the first moment I touched Ella in the way that lovers do, she was all I ever saw."

"My future path is set no matter my infatuation with Fiona. Kyla may have stood between her and I afore this day, but now Elizabeth does. The MacRae's daughter is an innocent lass and I proposed to her. I asked her to be my wife." He'd never backed down on his word once given yet, and he never intended to. He might no longer be honor-bound to wed Kyla, but he was honor-bound to wed Elizabeth.

Up ahead, the steep cliff side trail ran down toward Ardan and he slowed his mount as a lone horse's tracks in the trail up ahead seemed to halt then veer sharply into the woods.

He hauled his horse to a stop next to the clear hoof marks scored into the dusty ground and circled them.

Duncan pulled his mount in beside his, motioned with his head toward the forest. "The tracks dinnae continue on but instead cut away into the woods toward the village.

"Duncan!" A woman with glossy brown hair waved and galloped out from under the high arched gate. With pale blue breeches encasing her legs and a cream tunic peeking out from under the hem of her black riding jacket, she could be only one woman. Ella Matheson, his new sister.

His brother grinned from ear to ear beside him. Aye, definitely Ella.

"Gentlemen." Smiling, Ella brought her horse in between his and Duncan's destriers then reached across and cupped

Duncan's cheek. "I've missed you."

"I've missed you too, love." Duncan caught her hand and brought her fingers to his lips. "Meet my brother, Coll."

"Aye, 'tis clear to see you two are twins, although there is enough of a difference for me to easily tell you both apart." She nodded at him, gripped her reins tighter and edged her mount closer. "'Tis lovely to meet you, Coll."

"As it is to meet you." He patted his war horse's neck. "Welcome to the family."

"Thank you, although I've been told we now have quite the journey ahead of us. Hamish, the seer here at Ardan, foresaw your arrival and bade me to join you afore you made it inside. He 'saw' that you're searching for Fiona, although she's already ridden on to the village and now treks through the forested hills toward Loch Alsh and her father. Hamish insisted I'd be needed on your coming trip, that we're to make all haste and find her afore the midnight hour strikes this night."

"Did Hamish say whether or no' Fiona and Coll are mated?" Duncan narrowed his gaze on his wife.

"He wouldnae confirm or deny it, said only part of the journey in finding our chosen one belongs in the chase." She switched her gaze back to him. "Coll, Hamish also mentioned you're now betrothed to the Chief of MacRae's daughter, that he 'saw' that as well within his vision."

"Aye, I've signed a formal betrothal agreement with the MacRae and I'm set to wed Elizabeth at the end of this week."

"Oh, well, that might pose a bit of a problem if you're indeed mated to Fiona." She squeezed his arm. "But one I'm sure you'll handle considering our mated males always do."

"I'm no' mated to her." He couldn't keep the growl from his voice.

"I see." She cast a look at Duncan. "Your brother is much like you."

"You mean stubborn?"

"Aye, but he'll fall quickly into line once we catch her up." Chuckling, she patted the saddlebags strapped to her horse. "I've brought provisions in case this journey takes longer than we might hope for."

"A wise move." Duncan reached across and swung a satchel from Ella's shoulders and hooked the straps over his own shoulders then gestured toward the trail. "Ladies first, my love."

"Keep your gaze on the trail and no' on me. If you fall from your saddle again, I'm no' coming back to help you up." She shoved her knees into her mount's flanks and tore into the trees, her laugh floating back to them.

"Och, I'll never live that fall down will I?" his brother yelled to her then galloped off in fast pursuit.

He slapped his destrier's rear and bounded into the trees after Duncan. Find Fiona, he would, and afore the midnight hour struck this night. He'd always taken the fae seer's advice to heart, and didn't intend to ignore it now.

* * * *

As night loomed, the skies darkened overhead and the hilly forest pathway Fiona had trod by foot for hours, thickened even further. Branches scraped her arms and cheeks, while the brushwood spilled onto the trail and made the way through impassible.

Huffing, she halted and turned around in a slow circle. Not a break in the thick foliage overhead allowed the night sky to shine through. No moon or stars. Frustration and pain sliced through her, her satchel a heavy weight on her back and her empty water skin brushing against her hip where she'd belted it at her waist.

Trekking through the woods had always been an adventure, usually with Coll, Duncan, or Kyla at her side. This night though, 'twas no adventure at all, not when her very heart heaved with each step she took farther from the one man she'd never truly wanted to leave.

You'll know the moment when the intricate strands of the mated bond begin taking form between you. It's undeniable. You'll be driven toward him, and he'll be driven toward you, and since he's now touched you as you've said, well, that'll only make his chase of you even more intense. Kyla's words from this morning reverberated through her mind.

Aye, Kyla was right, and after having been touched so intimately by Coll last eve, it had most definitely increased her need for him. Her thoughts swarmed only with him. Certainly she no longer wished to continue on, not when her very soul demanded she return to him. She squeezed her eyes shut, hoped like hell these fierce emotions were taking Coll just as fiercely as they were taking her.

An owl hooted, the eerie call echoing through the towering trees and leafy undergrowth. She tipped her head toward the direction it had come from and caught the slight rush of water as she did. The river must be close. A river certainly ran right through this forest in a meandering line from Loch Alsh to Loch Carron. She grasped her red skirts dampened by the swirling forest mist and stumbled toward the river.

The splashing and gurgling thrummed louder and she picked up her pace, heaved branches aside and finally broke through the heavy tree line and lurched into a small clearing with the river snaking through it, the moon thankfully now a golden orb high above. Stars twinkled so prettily and never had she seen such a welcoming sight. Thank heavens she hadn't gotten herself completely lost, because if she didn't know where she was then how on earth would Coll know either.

Legs shaking, she staggered to the grassy edge of the bank and lowered to her knees, flipped her black cloak back and leaned in. Hands cupped, she scooped fresh water and with her palms lifted to her mouth, gulped it down. So good, yet also so chilly. The cold water hit her belly with an icy rush and goosebumps rippled across her skin.

No more for now. She'd fill her pouch and drink more later. Skin unplugged, she dipped it into the water, corked it once full and pushed to her feet. No farther would she walk this night. She'd make camp here and build a fire to keep warm by.

Satchel in hand, she clomped across to the nearest tree and propped it against the wide trunk. With her wrist dagger unsheathed, she crouched and loosened the soil with a few good stabs. She hollowed out a small pit, returned to the river bank and collected some stones then carefully stacked them in a circle around the pit.

After a short hunt within the nearest trees, she gathered sticks and a few pine cones then with the load of tinder in her arms, dropped what she'd collected next to the pit. A quick search netted her a large log which would burn for hours and knees locked tight, she dragged it back to her camp, scoring a trail in the leaf-strewn trail.

Sweat beaded and a trickle ran down her back, the work arduous but fulfilling and she set to work pulling stringy bark off the log in preparation to begin her fire. With flint from her pouch, she struck it with her dirk until a spark caught then hands scooped around the tiny flame, she coaxed it into life and only once assured the fire had truly taken ahold, added twigs and then the large log until it blazed.

Huddled in front of the fire's crackling warmth on her plaid, she rubbed her chilled hands together. Sixteen months ago, the night before Coll's leaving, she'd sat around just such a fire as this one. He'd asked her to meet him before they'd parted ways and she had, in the woods near their pool. Before the brilliant flicker of the fire's orange and yellow flames, he'd spread out a blanket and motioned for her to join him.

In her blue kirtle, she'd plopped down and stretched out her legs, while a frisky wind had breezed through and along with it had brought the sweet fragrance from the lavender bushes clumped amongst the surrounding pine trees. The splashing of the waterfall hitting the pool rushed from close by, although that special place remained just beyond her sight.

"There is naught I love more than being outside under a night sky." Both hating and desiring these final few hours with him, she'd flopped onto her back and stared up at the darkened sky with its myriad of twinkling stars blazing above.

"I wholeheartedly agree." In his black leather pants and a billowy white tunic, he'd laid down side to side with her and stared up at the same sky as she did. *"You'll make a fine wife for Matthew."*

"Ha, that I didnae expect you to say." She couldn't help but smile, no matter the difficult beginning to their conversation. *"Tell me what you're feeling."*

"There is no other choice left to you, and I understand that." Solemn words.

"I see." She'd rolled onto her side and fully faced him, the distance between them a mere foot or two, yet the divide couldn't have felt greater. *"Look at me."*

He'd rolled onto his side too, caught her hand and trapped her fingers against the heat of his chest. With his gaze locked on hers, he'd breathed slowly in and out.

So did she, her thoughts so scrambled, and for some time all they did was lie there like that and take in the moment. That had been a sliver of time she'd never get back, and so she'd memorized every detail of his face, from the rich brown shade of his eyes with those stunning flecks of gold, to the dimples either side of his lush lips, and the deep cleft in his chin holding a razz of stubble. If only she could get past the natural barrier in his mind and read his emotions too. She'd love naught more than to know exactly what he was thinking and feeling since he hadn't shared much.

"You're tapping at my mind." He'd stroked the back of one finger along her cheek. *"I can sense it."*

"Then lower your shields so I no longer have to."

"If I released my emotions right now, you'd get swamped in them." He'd leaned in closer, touched the tip of his nose to hers. *"I also prefer it that you cannae sense my emotions most of the time."*

"I'm sure you do." Eyes closed, she'd reached out with her fae empath ability and tried harder to capture even just one of his current thoughts or feelings, but there was nothing. She growled under her breath. *"Your fae blood annoys me this night."*

"As yours usually annoys me most of the time too." With his hand on her waist, he rubbed his thumb in a slow circle over her hip, his touch pure magic, settling and soothing her frustration so swiftly. *"'Tis also at times like these when you mention my fae blood that my thoughts always return to the night when I first learnt of my true birthmother. Eight, I'd been at the time, and in Father's solar. I'll never forget when I noticed you hiding under the table. I caught sight of your toes peeking out from under the tablecloth and knew 'twas you."*

"I'd snuck in earlier, when the fae woman from the Matheson village arrived with Kyla. The woman's emotions had rolled out in strong waves to me, and she'd clearly been worried about you and Duncan as well, although I didnae know why. That I had to learn the answer to." She'd been right to sneak in that night, for that had been when Coll and Duncan had learnt that the woman who'd arrived, Grace Matheson, had been a dear friend of their true birthmother's. Grace had held the skill of death-warning and seen trouble was about to befall Coll and Duncan, so she'd brought them a message so they might survive. That night they'd learnt of their true fae heritage, that their fae battle skill would soon come into being.

"Grace is the one who forced Father to admit the truth to Duncan and I, and to explain why he'd kept the secret of who our true mother was to himself for the first eight years of our lives."

"I'm so glad Grace came that night." Grace, Kyla's true

mother, was such a sweet woman.

"So am I, although no' for Kyla's sake. That was when Father became intrigued by her. Only a few days later, he stole into her parents' village and spirited her away. She'd been so young at the time, torn away from her kin, and never to see them again. That pained me greatly."

"As it did me, and I wish we could see Kyla safely back home to her parents now."

"She willnae leave us, no' when Father has always held the safety of her parents over her head. He'll slaughter each and every one of those from within her fae village should she attempt to return." He'd squeezed her hip, his fingers going in tight. *"Do you recall Grace's decree that night?"*

"I'll never forget it." Grace had told Coll and Duncan that their destiny was to ensure that the fae lived, and they'd taken her words to heart. She cupped his cheek, grazed her fingers along his skin. *"Make our clan great for our future kin, Coll."*

"Duncan and I intend to."

His words from that night haunted her still, yet she'd also accepted his future would be with Kyla, and hers with Matthew, or at least until this night.

Kyla had now been found by her mate and they'd spoken vows. Ronan had also made certain those at the fae village—including Kyla's parents—had been made aware of Colin MacKenzie's threat. They all took the greatest of care and ensured their full security, so should there ever be a strike by Colin at their village, then they'd be fully prepared for it. An answer to their dreams.

"Fiona?" Something white flashed beyond the fire, there one moment and gone the next.

She scuttled back, until her back hit the wide trunk. Hands gripping the rough bark behind her, she shoved to her feet clawing upward. Heartbeat a racing mess, she searched the darkened trees. "Who goes there?"

"I'm Cherub, the guardian of my fae kind." The faerie's voice wisped all about within the nighttime breeze then she appeared from the misty dark and took her full form, her white fur hooded cloak swishing back from her shoulders over top of a regal blue gown, her hands tucked within the rounded warmth of a white fur muff dangling from her neck. With a soft smile, Cherub eyed her. "Well, glad I am to finally meet you, Fiona MacKenzie."

Their fae princess was actually here? And talking to her?

She gulped, her throat so dry. Of course she'd heard of the legend surrounding Cherub, that she could manipulate her element of air, both cloak herself and become as one with it by taking on a mist form. Yet naught could have ever prepared her for this meeting, at this very moment.

"You appear stunned." Cherub's blond hair whipped all about her, her skin sparkling as if touched by the very stars themselves, all glittery and dazzling.

"I—I—" Her tongue got stuck to the roof of her mouth. "Legend says you've lived over a thousand years, that you can open portals and travel through time. Is it true?"

"Aye, I'm an immortal time-walker and aid my people wherever and however I can, whether that be in the future or far in the past." She pulled her hands from the muff and swished them through the air. A wicker basket materialized out of nowhere and floated toward her. "This is for you."

"Oh my." The basket bumped softly down on the grass at her feet and no matter how many times she blinked, it remained right there. "Where did this come from, and how did you do that?"

"It's come from my mate's twenty-first century time, and 'tis a little trick I've learnt over the centuries. 'Tis wonderful to meet you, Fiona, and this basket of goodies is for you. I've just spoken to Kyla, gave her quite the surprise when I did. She told me of what happened between you and Coll last eve, although

I'm no' surprised to learn of it." Smiling rather mischievously, Cherub lifted her hands into the air again and swirled the wind once more. It whipped about, sent the fire's flames soaring higher and the branches overhead swaying. The grass rippled in all directions and the river water churned as it flowed faster downstream. "'Tis time for Coll and you to both accept your destiny. No more will I permit him to ignore your mated bond. He allowed you to wed another, even now intends on speaking vows with a lass he does no' care for, and that I cannae permit. Setting you aside a second time is unacceptable, and since you've begun the hunt, you must now ensure he sees it fully through."

"I may have begun this chase, but he's so very stubborn and—and—are you certain we're mated?" She clutched her chest, her hope so high. If anyone could confirm their bond existed, it would be Cherub.

"Very certain, although I fear he'll never choose you when his honor is at stake. In his eyes, his duty to his clan must prevail and even though he is now honor-bound to wed Elizabeth MacRae, the lass is still no' for him. Dinnae give up on him, but embrace this new challenge in your life. He is certainly a man driven this night and rides this way as we speak, right along with Duncan and Ella." Cherub lifted a few inches from the ground and swept backward. "I must go afore he arrives, but within the basket you'll find some treats to enjoy." Cherub blew her a kiss and just as quickly as she'd come, shimmered away within the swirling wind.

The breeze calmed, so swiftly, and the pounding of horses' hooves echoed toward her.

She hurried to the center of the clearing and through the dense line of the darkened trees, three riders broke free, their mounts snorting misty air. Coll at the front, then Duncan and Ella right behind him.

They pulled their horses to a halt, grim anger slashing

Coll's face, the emotion pulsing through the air and smothering her. Wonderful, so now he shared his emotions. Well, he was about to get a handful of her own too. Cherub had decreed they were soul bound, which meant she needed him to accept that fact as well.

With a fierce bellow, Coll bounded from his destrier and stormed toward her. He planted his feet wide, slapped his hands on his sides and sent her yet another whirlwind of his wrath. "Woman, you cannae simply ride from my keep and cross these mountains without a guard."

"I know this land as well as you do, Coll MacKenzie." She'd certainly never tell him she'd gotten lost, because well, she barely had gotten lost and that's all that counted. What also counted was the fact he'd come after her. She'd instigated the hunt, and he'd begun the chase. "Although I do appreciate that you're now here."

"Appreciate?" Another bellowing word.

"Coll, please, I am no' a simpering lass who you can berate however you wish." She jabbed a finger into his chest, his very big and immoveable chest. "How could you agree to wed another lass without speaking to me about it first? Explain that."

"I am no' a man who you can berate however you wish either. Nor must I clear all my doings with you first." His dark war coat studded with bits of steel flapped open at his sides and gave a glimpse of his lethally sharp blade sheathed at his hip. "Last I heard, you belonged to Matthew, and I'd had no knowledge of that changing."

"I've never belonged to Matthew. He never once demanded marital rights or even bestowed more than a kiss on my cheek, whereas your coming marriage to Elizabeth MacRae will be consummated in every way."

"I cannae set Elizabeth aside simply because you and I have touched."

"Excuse me." Duncan dismounted and swung Ella down

from her steed, their horses whinnying. "You two clearly need some privacy for this argument you're having."

"There is no argument," Coll snapped back at him.

"Aye, there is." His brother collected their horses' reins, looped their leads to a boulder near the stream then scooped Ella into his arms. "Do excuse us. We have some of our own arguing to undertake."

"Oooh, I do love a good arguing session with you." Ella wrapped her arms around Duncan's neck and nipped his ear. "You are about to get an ear-lashing."

"One with all the right noises, I hope." Grinning, Duncan jogged off with her into the trees and the two disappeared.

"You should never have walked into my bedchamber last eve." Coll leaned closer, the muscle in his jaw thumping a hard and fast beat.

She breathed out, tried to center herself then once assured she could speak calmly, met his irrefutable gaze. "You cannae marry Elizabeth MacRae. I willnae allow it."

"You have no right to say who I can or cannae marry." Slowly, he circled her, his gaze roaming down her body, from her head to the low neckline of her gown then her hips, legs and back up again.

She followed his very predatory move, his hands clenching and unclenching at his sides, his brown leather pants hugging his muscular legs and his white tunic flapping freely under his coat. "Do you like what you see?" She planted her own hands on her hips. "My stubborn one."

"What happened between us last eve should never have happened." He halted in front of her. "I touched you in ways I had no right to."

"You had every right considering our mated bond."

"There is no bond, and if I'd known about Matthew's death at the time, or that I wasn't dreaming but you were actually there in my chamber, then we would never have even kissed."

"Are you angry at me for speaking vows with Matthew?" He had every right to be now she'd been made aware of their bond. Yet at the time, she'd seen no other way past their issues. Her father had threatened that she must choose a husband soon, or if she didn't, then he'd have chosen one for her. So too Coll's father wouldn't have waited forever before finally demanding his son wed Kyla, and Coll had been the most obvious choice from amongst their chief's three sons. Their chief certainly wished to ensure that only the strongest fae blood continued to flow through his direct line, and Kyla's was as strong as it could possibly come.

"To begin with, aye, but I soon recognized he was the best choice for you."

"Matthew suffered such deep depression. He should never have passed away from the small arm wound he'd taken in training, but it festered and he succumbed so quickly." She'd never told another soul, but she'd caught Matthew deepening his wound with his own dirk, almost slicing right across his wrist. He'd been deep within a fever at the time and thrashing about in his sickbed. In his hazed grief for Elspeth, he'd looked at her and even called her by his dead wife's name. His last words had been a promise to his beloved, that he'd join her now and not wait another day. Then he'd stabbed himself right in the belly and with his immense strength, she'd been unable to halt his hand. His blood had flowed like an endless river across the grooves in his torso, then trickled from his mouth. Tears had burned behind her eyes. She'd failed Matthew.

Her pain and heartache from that day swarmed her now.

Living without the one their heart desired was sheer torture, and she had no desire to continue living an empty and lonely life without Coll any longer. "I want you, Coll. You hold the other half of my soul, just as I hold the other half of yours and even Cherub, our fae princess, has declared that is so. She visited me here, mere minutes ago, even left me a basket of treats from her chosen one's twenty-first century time." She gestured to the basket. "I didnae leave Carron Castle with that."

"Cherub's truly been here?" He lifted a brow, his brown eyes darkening. "As in the guardian to our fae people? You've truly seen her?"

"She is real, and told me 'twas time for you to accept your destiny, that since I've begun the hunt, you must see the chase through. Please say you believe me."

"I proposed to another woman. If I was mated to you, I'd never have been able to do so. That is the only truth that matters."

"I understand you wish to secure a stronger alliance with the Chief of MacRae, but surely there is another way."

"The only way is through marriage vows, and I'll be speaking them with Elizabeth by the week's end. The future safety of our clan depends upon it."

"And what of my feelings for you?" She stepped around him, tugged his war coat off his shoulders and down his arms.

"What are you doing?" His muscles tensed, biceps rippling under the thin white cloth of his tunic.

"Undressing you. I need to show you how very deep my feelings run. I wish to seduce you." She dropped his coat on the ground next to her satchel. "We can complete the bond here if you wish. Duncan and Ella willnae return unless one of us calls out to them."

"I willnae allow any form of seduction to occur between us, and I meant it when I said there was no bond." He reached for his coat but she stepped into his way.

"You are so terribly stubborn." She gripped the dangling ties of his tunic where the deep V collar lay loosely laced and tugged on them. "No more fighting, Coll. We've denied this bond for years, but no longer can we do so. You're the only one I've ever desired."

"That desire is called lust, no' the mated bond." The breeze lifted his shirt hem and gave a mouth watering show of his golden skin and the roped muscles either side of his abs.

"Kiss me." She leaned into him, brushed her chest against his. Seduce him she would, without another moment's delay.

"I intend on taking you back to Ardan where you can stay with Duncan and Ella. You're not to continue on to your father's home since he'll have you wed to another man afore too long. You'll be safe with Duncan. He'll never allow any harm to come to you."

"I said kiss me."

"You're no' listening, Fiona." He pushed her back against the tree and shoved his heavenly body up hard against hers. "There is no bond."

"All I understand is that you're saying one thing with your mouth, and another with your body. You clearly wish to keep me close. Put your hands on me, anywhere you please. My body is yours, my heart is yours, and my soul will be yours throughout all eternity. I give myself freely to you."

"My betrothal is as binding as a marriage contract can be." Such agony crossed his face, and his pained emotions slammed into her, over and over. Never had he allowed her to sense his feelings so deeply before, and it meant the world to her that he now did. She would try and ease his agony, and with the truth no less.

"You are all I've ever desired, all I've ever wished for. Never have I understood Matthew's great pain so deeply until now." She too would never survive his death should it occur. "Make love to me, claim my body and fuse the golden strands of our mated bond fully together."

"I've signed a damned agreement and there is naught I can do to end my betrothal."

"Are you asking me to let you go again?"

"I've never been yours to let go."

"Aye, that is exactly what you're asking then." Her tears

fell. Giving him up a second time would destroy her, all of her.

* * * *

"Dinnae cry. Please, dinnae cry." Fiona's pain gripped Coll's heart like a fist and naught could stem the pressure unless he—aye, he needed to kiss her. He dipped his head and touched his mouth to hers. He wanted to kiss her softly and cherish this moment, but instead the renewed taste of her sent his senses swirling into a maelstrom.

They couldn't be soul bound, but they were most definitely attracted to each other. Aye, this was lust and he simply needed to expend it. Pulling back a touch, he looked deep into her eyes and when another tear slid free down her cheek, his chest near collapsed in on itself. He captured her mouth again and kissed her ravenously, with all the desperate desire and need to see those tears gone.

"Aye, give me more of your kisses. I'll take whatever you're willing to offer for now." She rocked her hips against his hips and his cock swelled painfully as the pressure to take her and truly make her his roared through him. Nay, he couldn't give into his own base desires, not when doing so would mean he'd fail his people. Those at Carron remained under his protection and must always come first, not his own needs or desires.

"I adore your kisses, Coll." Whispered words against his lips.

As he adored hers and hell, if he could just lessen this edge of hunger riding him so hard, then mayhap he'd be able to think more clearly afterward. It didn't help that she was wearing his gift, the red velvet gown he'd had the seamstress fashion for her. He stroked the soft fabric at her hips, the color bringing out the red highlights in her silky locks and the flush stealing across the upper swells of her breasts. Aye, he'd held those full mounds in his hands last eve and tasted the sweet treasure of them too. Mayhap one more time.

He plucked the front laces of her cinched bodice loose and

the low neckline embroidered with white detailing drooped open and exposed a slight tease of her pink nipples. Gently, he eased his hand fully inside the bodice, soft velvet sliding sensuously across the back of his hand and with a staggered breath, he palmed her lush flesh. "I shouldnae be touching you so."

"You may touch me as freely as you wish. I'm yours and there's no part of me I'd now keep from you." She pressed his hands tighter against her breasts, until the heavy beat of her heart pulsed against his palms. "My heart is yours, Coll. My soul is yours, and I wish for my body to be yours as well."

"I cannae take any more from you than I already have." He swiped both his thumbs over her nipples and they puckered all pink and tight. Not enough. He needed to touch more of her. He shoved the sleeves of her gown down her arms and exposed her creamy skin bathed in the golden glow of the moon. His mind hazed with lust and he bent and licked one nipple then gently blew across it until it stiffened even further.

"Mmm, do that again," she whimpered, clutching his shirtfront.

"You should be telling me to halt." Slowly, carefully, he drew one bud deep inside his mouth and tickled the tip with his tongue. Hell, she tasted divine, like the sweetest nectar of the sweetest fruit. More. He tweaked her other nipple then laved and treasured it, just as he'd done with the first.

"Dinnae stop, Coll." Eyes closed, she arched her back and he scooped her up and laid her down on her plaid before the fire. She smiled, so damn seductively and he got lost.

"I love the way you're looking at me."

"I love the way you're looking at me too." She tugged the ties of his pants loose and grinned as his cock bobbed free.

"Wait." A grating request.

"Nay, I'm done waiting, my stubborn one." She curled her fingers around his shaft and gripped him as if she owned him, which right now she surely did.

"Halt," he croaked, the plea barely making it past his lips. "I'll come in an instant if you continue to touch me there."

"That's exactly what I'd like, for you to come and to never forget either me or my touch." She swiped one finger over the head of his cock and his shaft pulsed in her hand, so greedy for more.

"Fiona, I cannae give you any more than this one moment in time." He dropped his head to her neck and sucked on the sensitive skin where her shoulder and neck met.

"Even though I want all of you, I'll agree to whatever you're willing to offer right now."

"I still shouldnae be doing this." Yet he captured her mouth again and kissed her, as if his very life depended upon it. These past sixteen months while she'd been beyond his reach at Rhue had near killed him, and now she was here and no longer wed to Matthew, 'twas a dream come true. He bunched up her skirts, slid his hand between her legs and nudged them farther apart. "I'm going to touch you below. Say aye."

"Aye." She fisted his shaft tighter and he rocked deeper into her exquisite hold and groaned, his need to take all she offered riding him hard.

"You are more than a wicked temptress." He cupped her mound, slowly stroked along her hot folds then caressed her nub which had her gripping him tighter and gasping with pleasure. "Matthew never touched you here did he?" He nipped her ear, needing to know for certain. "Tell me he didnae."

"He was in love with Elspeth, would never have touched me when all he desired was her. He was always the consummate gentleman." Breasts heaving, the fiery light in her blue eyes bright with fierce passion, she whispered, "What of you? Have you ever touched another woman as you're touching me?"

When he'd tried to touch Elizabeth and offer her a kiss, he'd only ended up backing away when his gut had soured and bile had risen. "Nay."

"There is a reason why, and 'tis called the mated bond." She glanced down between their bodies at his hand underneath her skirts. "Which means if you even try to stop touching me right now, I'm going to get very angry."

"Then this kind of touch pleases you, my fiery empath?" He slanted his mouth over hers, plunged one finger deep inside her hot channel and kissed her with all the heated desire that drove him. This woman had always held a piece of his heart and although he was certain no soul bond existed as she'd said, she'd always been the one bright star in his life. Always and forever. Caressing her, he stroked ever deeper inside her then pulled out and smoothed over her nub before sliding deep into her core once again.

"Oooh, that feels—oh goodness, it feels—" She pumped him harder. "I willnae come without you."

"I cannae hold on much longer." He added a second finger into her tight channel and stretched her wider. "Tell me if I bring you any pain."

"There is only pleasure. I promise you, only pleasure." She spread her fingers over him like a claiming and a heavy pressure buzzed at the base of his spine, the tingle heating to a fierce burn that roared around to the front and pulsed through his cock.

Kissing her, he moaned into her mouth and she raised her hips and shuddered in his arms, her inner core dragging his fingers ever deeper inside her and he exploded, his essence spurting from him across the grass. Over and over, he came, and naught had ever felt so very right. Holding her, touching her, consumed his very soul.

"So magical," she murmured against his lips. "Now let's do that again, but this time you come inside me. I want your cock buried deep within. That is the only way to fully cement our bond."

Chapter 4

Unadulterated pleasure had raced through Fiona as Coll's cock had throbbed in her hand. He'd touched her, so intimately and her inner channel had pulsed around his fingers. More than anything she'd wanted him to claim her fully, for him to join them in the way of those within the bond.

"We're not doing this again." Gruff words as he continued to gently caress her within. "Are you all right?"

"I'm wonderful, but could of course be better. Come inside me, please."

"What I need to do is put some distance between us." Chest heaving and his breath still coming fast, he pitched to his side and flopped onto his back next to her. One long minute passed before he moved, then when he did it wasn't to pull her into his arms as she'd hoped. Instead, he righted his pants, fixed her skirts and bodice with a brisk touch then crawled even farther away to the other side of the fire. Once there, he moved into a crouch as if unsure whether he wished to bolt or not.

"Stay." She pushed herself upright into a seated position and searched his gaze. "Tell me what you're thinking."

"I never intended for what just happened, to happen. You make me lose all rational thought." He glanced into the darkened tree line. "I certainly didnae ride out after you this day so I might ravish you again once I'd found you."

"I wanted to be ravished, still want to be ravished."

"So I noticed." He gritted his teeth, in that way he always did when he got completely obstinate. "'Tis been a long day and we both need some time apart. Wait here while I find Duncan and Ella." He heaved to his feet and stormed into the trees.

"Coll, wait!" But he didn't. He disappeared so fast.

Damn it. How frustrating. This bond could be so annoying and completely aggravating, and why on earth had she been given such a stubborn mate? First, her chosen one had been honor-bound to wed Kyla, and now he remained honor-bound to wed the Chief of MacRae's daughter.

'Tis time for Coll and you to both accept your destiny. No more will I permit him to ignore your mated bond. He allowed you to wed another, even now intends on speaking vows with a lass he does no' care for, and that I cannae permit. Setting you aside a second time is unacceptable, and since you've begun the hunt, you must now ensure he sees it fully through.

Cherub's words echoed through her mind.

Aye, she'd continue the hunt, and force Coll to see this chase through.

She shoved to her feet, snatched her satchel, slung it over one shoulder then with the sides of her black fur cloak pulled tighter around her, stormed off into the dark. She marched toward Loch Carron and back toward Coll's land. Aye, no more would she travel toward her father, not when he'd soon see her wed to another man and that she couldn't have.

She followed the river as it weaved deep through the woods, Cherub's words continuing to thrum strongly through her mind and giving her the determination she needed to force each foot before the other, even though the last thing she wished to do was leave Coll behind.

Riled, she stomped along the mossy edge of the river bank

and the mushy ground sucked at her booted feet.

Through the dense and darkened woods, she pushed on with only the barest trace of moonlight now breaking through the thick canopy overhead.

Finally, an hour or two later, the river widened and the crashing tumble of a waterfall traveled toward her.

She hastened her pace and stumbled to a stop as she emerged at the rocky cliff face where the river cascaded over slick black boulders, streamed over the edge of the falls and crashed into a ravine a hundred feet below. White water surged and frothed within the pool and flowed onward downstream.

Hands on her hips, she teetered on the very edge of the craggy rise overlooking the moonlit valley far below. The glorious sight of the inner channel of Loch Carron winding its way inland with the odd wattle-and-daub longhouse nestled along its length, calmed her. This land belonged to Coll and Duncan. They'd made their claim here, and one day Coll would be the Chief of Clan MacKenzie in this beautiful place, and she wished to be right here with him when that day arrived.

Crouching, she pressed one hand to the slick black rock. To her left, a steep trail led down toward the lower land and within the basin of the valley, a stone tavern she'd yet to visit peeked out from within a stand of towering elm trees, smoke puffing from its high chimney. She'd seek shelter there for the night, await Coll's arrival while she—

"Fiona!" Coll's shout pierced through the crashing of the waterfall.

"Fiona!" Duncan and Ella's shouts ricocheted toward her too.

Well, well. He'd arrived already. This chase was moving along nicely. Hands curved around her mouth, she called back, "I'm here."

Coll crashed out of the trees with his horse's reins in hand, his beast clomping behind him. With his dark hair all mussed and those stunning sparks of gold rimming his brown eyes glowing an almost feral color, he advanced on her. "You. Left. Me. Again."

"You gave me no choice." She took a step back and wobbled as stones sheared away from the cliff edge and rapped down the rock face.

"I've got you." He swung her in beside him, his hands a little shaky. "You need to take more care where you step. If you'd fallen"—he kissed her hard—"I'd never have forgiven myself."

"About time we found you." Duncan led his horse out of the trees, the wicker basket Cherub had gifted her swinging from one hand.

"Aye, any longer and Coll would have torn these woods apart." Ella walked out with her mount beside her, her relief evident in her soulful fae eyes. "Are you making your way back to Ardan or Carron?"

"Carron, and I just spied an inn below, thought it would make a fine place to seek shelter for the night."

"Wonderful." Ella stepped forward in her leather boots laced snugly all the way to her knees over her blue breeches. She hugged her. "'Tis late and I would love naught more than a soft bed to rest in for the night."

"As would I." Duncan snuck Ella's reins from her and tipped his head toward the steep downward trail. "You move ahead first. Watch your step. I'll follow."

"I agree to going first, but keep your gaze off my backside and on the trail. No missing a step yourself." Ella tweaked Duncan's chin and with a giggle, disappeared down the steep trail lined with thick scrub on one side and the rocky cliff face on the other.

"I'll look wherever I please, my love." Duncan followed her, his chuckle floating back to her and Coll.

"Fiona." Coll slanted his head at her, the fiery look in his eyes one she'd seen a time or two, one which meant a showdown was about to occur, and clearly currently between them. She could handle such though, was fully prepared for it. "In the morn, I'm taking you back to Ardan House, not Carron," he muttered. "You'll be safe with Duncan and Ella, because I'm certainly done with chasing you across these hills."

"Why no' your home?"

"Because my betrothed is due to arrive any day. We'll be married by the end of the week."

"If I return to Ardan with Duncan and Ella, then it willnae be for long." Never could she remain so close to Carron if he did in fact speak vows with Elizabeth MacRae, although she wasn't giving up the battle yet.

"And where will you go?" He snarled under his breath, the fierce sound rumbling within the darkened pull of the night.

"I certainly dinnae intend to marry a second time." She shuddered at the thought of that. Aye, she'd considered her options often over the course of the past few months while at Carron as she'd awaited his return. Following Kyla's marriage, she'd intended on speaking to Coll and telling him how deeply she loved him, had always loved him, and if he decided to spurn that love, then she'd thought it best for her to retire to the nunnery on the Isle of Iona. "I wish to use my empath ability to aid others, in whatever way that might be needed. My cousin has taken her vows at the abbey on Iona and she and I have always been close. I will have kin nearby if I join her there, and that is important to me. Does that arrangement suit you?" Let him see if he'd allow that.

The tic was back to pulsing in his jaw. "A nunnery is no place for you."

"'Tis said no men are permitted within the abbey's walls." She would fight for him, push him however she could to get him to see reason.

"Aye, you'd forever remain beyond my reach."

"Then are we agreed on the abbey?" She extended her hand, held it out for him to shake.

"I'd no longer be able to even speak with you." He glared at her hand.

"Surely that sounds like a blessing, hmmm?" She raised a brow, pushed her hand out further. "Since you insist we arena soul bound and all."

"I will never agree to you entering Iona Abbey." Snapping his teeth together, he swept her up in his arms and tossed her over his shoulder.

Her belly thumped into his rock hard shoulder and her breath whooshed from her. "Coll MacKenzie, put me down."

"You've been beyond my reach for the past sixteen months and now that you're right here with me, you speak of entering a damn nunnery." He clamped one hand over the backs of her legs as he stormed down the steep incline, his horse clomping behind him with naught but a short whistle issued. "You'll stay at Ardan with Duncan and Ella, and go nowhere else. Am I understood?"

"Please, be careful. I dinnae wish for you to topple over the side of this cliff and take me with you when you do. I value my life." She thumped his backside since it swayed within easy reach, her red hair dangling down to his knees. Oh, and what a fine looking backside he had too. So deliciously firm and when she smoothed one hand over each of his tight cheeks, she struggled to draw in a decent breath.

"Fiona." One low growl.

"Aye, my mate."

"There is a grave difference between knowing I cannae see you, and knowing I'll never see you." He stomped onward.

"I harbor the same fear when it comes to you. You intend on speaking vows with another woman and if you do, I'll never forgive you." Such a heavy ache throbbed in her heart. "You walked away from me sixteen months ago, left me without once looking back, and I'd honestly harbored the hope back then that you'd ride in and halt my marriage to Matthew from occurring."

"I agreed to wed Elizabeth afore I ever knew of your widowed state." Pain laced each of his words, his grip on her legs tightening. "And I couldnae return to you and halt your marriage to Matthew when my marriage to Kyla was all but inevitable. I couldnae forsake her."

"Yet you'll forsake me now, your own soul bound mate."

"You arenae my mate." He bounded from the trail onto the flat land, drew his horse around then slung her from his shoulder straight into his destrier's saddle. She landed with a creak of the leather and her hair all a-tumble about her face.

Shoving it back, she glared at him. "We are mated," she huffed. "You've been chasing me all day and there is only one reason for you to do so."

"Aye, and it's called halting your madness so you willnae get hurt." He bounded in behind her in one swift jump, wrapped his arms about her waist and gripping the reins, nodded at Duncan and Ella now mounted on their own steeds. "Let's ride."

"Oh, you are so beyond infuriating." And right now she was too damn tired to keep arguing with him, so instead she leaned back against his chest and sank into the undeniable warmth of his hold as he thrust his knees into his destrier's flanks and rode toward the inn after Duncan and Ella.

So much for Cherub's decree that they were soul bound. Even though 'twas true, it had made little difference to Coll when she'd said it. Damn his unbending honor and inability to accept a bond had formed between them.

"You've gone suddenly quiet. Is all well?" He nipped her ear from behind, his voice a husky murmur. "You're one of my dearest friends, Fiona. I hate to see you so upset."

"You believe we're just friends?" Shuffling around, she glared at him some more.

"Aye." A firm nod.

"You're fighting our bond, telling yourself it does no' exist, and I want to be more than one of your dearest friends. I want to be your mate, your wife, your lover and the keeper of your very heart and soul."

"Then you strive for too much." He looked ahead and urged his horse to a faster pace. Duncan and Ella galloped several horse lengths ahead. They rounded the bend in the trail and disappeared through the gates into the tavern's inner courtyard.

Stubborn, stubborn man. Goodness. In the past, whenever he'd decided to dig in his heels in such a way, it had always been near impossible to make him change his mind. Which was right now the case as well. "I detest that you willnae see reason."

"As I detest that you willnae either." He slowed his horse and trotted through the tavern's gates and past an herb garden. The fragrant mint and wild garlic swirled within the night air then wafted away as they clomped across the gravelly yard to where Duncan and Ella had already dismounted next to stables.

A stable hand ducked out from within the darkened interior and took Duncan and Ella's horses then steered their mounts inside.

Duncan swept one arm around Ella's waist and guided her across the front yard and through the inn's door with its low hung eaves and stony facade.

Behind her, Coll brought their mount to a halt near the corral, tossed one leg over and landed on the ground with a *thump*. Hands on her waist, he lifted her free and set her down between him and his horse. Keeping her firmly close, he tossed a coin to the lad and muttered, "See that these three horses are well cared for. Ensure they have an extra hand of oats as well. They've been ridden hard this day."

"Right away, my laird." With splotchy red cheeks and grass-strained elbows, the boy wearing brown breeches and a tunic with the sleeves rolled up, guided their horse into the stables.

"Inside with you now." Coll picked up her wicker basket

where Duncan had set it down near the round corral post and with their bags strung over his shoulder, he gestured her toward the tavern.

She grasped her red skirts and walked around a lanky brown-haired dog in the center of the yard and ducked inside under the eaves. Inside the main room, a fire blazed within the hearth, a most welcoming heat which she embraced after the chill of the night outside.

Behind her, Coll stepped in and ran one hand gently down her back. "Have you been here afore?"

"Nay, but 'tis so quaint and lovely." Wooden screens separated the central tables where patrons partook of the hearty stew and tankards of ale. Soft chatter filled the roomy space with its latticed windows overlooking the rolling moors and the meandering length of Loch Carron beyond. In the moonlight, the darkened waters glistened a golden hue.

"I've stayed here once afore, on one of my trips to the markets," Ella said as she tucked a lock of her glossy brown hair behind one ear. Duncan dipped his nose into her locks and kissed her lobe. She giggled and curled one hand around the back of his head, murmured. "I take it you'd like a room for the night right now, my mate?"

"I'd sleep with you anywhere, in a bed or outside under the stars, although only once I've fed you." Duncan nipped her lips. "Your belly is rumbling and you must be hungry."

"That," Coll bit out in her ear, "is the mated bond, one which we dinnae have."

"So you say, and so I disagree." She gave him her own biting words back, wished she could nip his ear too.

Coll stalked across to the bar where the innkeeper, a stocky man with loose breeches and a plaid tossed over one shoulder, dried tankards with his cloth. "Gordon." Coll acknowledged the man with a firm nod and hand extended. "'Tis good to see you again."

"My laird." The bald-headed man shook Coll's hand with hearty enthusiasm. "'Tis good to see you've returned safely from your travels to the north. The wife has seafood stew cooking, as well as more loaves of fresh bread warm from the oven. Do ye require rooms for the night?"

"Seafood stew and fresh bread would be greatly appreciated. Rooms as well. We're in need of three if you have them."

"I've two rooms which I'll have the maids ready for ye immediately, both side by side above-stairs, and the third willnae be far away." Find yourselves somewhere to sit and I'll see to your meals first." The innkeeper bustled through the kitchen door and the hearty aroma of the stew wafted through.

Removing her black cloak and draping it over one arm, she joined Coll. "I can sleep outside if needed. He does no' need to find me a third room."

"There isnae a chance I'll allow you to sleep outside. I want you in the chamber next to mine, right where I'll hear you if you attempt to leave. Duncan and Ella will take the third room once it's been readied for them."

"I had intended on sleeping outside had it no' been for your arrival at my camp."

"You desired the chase, Fiona. You knew I'd come for you."

"If you're referring to the chase of the mated bond, then aye, I will never deny that I invoked it."

"There is no blasted"—he lowered his voice to a rough whisper—"bond. The chase I simply referred to was the one across my land to catch you afore some villain did."

"If you could just admit the truth, then that would go halfway toward helping matters." Huffing, she pushed a finger against his chest, one sleeve slipping from her shoulder. She went to open her mouth to argue her point further, only his gaze slid to her breasts and the gaping neckline of her gown. He gulped, his throat working hard as he gripped her sleeve and smoothed it back into place. Lifting his gaze back to hers, such a deep hunger swirled within, one which she wanted him to release, desperately. "Admit there's a bond, Coll, and I'm all yours."

"Enough." He set a hand to the small of her back and ushered her across the room to the table in the far corner under the window. He pulled out the bench, pressed her shoulders until she sat then eased in beside her.

Duncan and Ella took the bench seat opposite them.

"Here ye are, my lovelies. This should slake your thirst." A barmaid bounced in, a tray of tankards in hand, the dangerously low neckline of her blue kirtle almost causing her breasts to spill forth. The wench leaned in and gave Coll a rather stunning eyeful of her bountiful flesh and a flare of jealousy reared so swift and sharp within her.

Oh goodness. That jealousy would arise far stronger if she ever met his bride-to-be.

"Thank you, Edana." Coll smiled at the hussy and she wanted to stab her.

"My laird, 'tis so good to see ye've returned." In a near purr, the maid leaned in even farther. "One of the other maids will be out with your meals shortly, although you be sure to holler out if ye need aught more from me. I've willing hands for whatever task ye have need to put them to."

"Go on with you." Coll swatted her bottom and Edana squealed and bounced away to the next table.

"Your meals, my laird." Another serving lass joined them with a platter of bannocks that had been baked and accompanied with wedges of cheese, while a second maid with an apron tied around her waist brought out a tray holding bowls of stew. The two young lasses passed one to each of them, laid out spoons and with bright smiles, whisked back to the kitchens.

Coll slid his dagger from its wrist sheath, sliced the

bannocks and passed her a piece. "Eat and warm your belly."

"Thank you," she grumped, then stuck the flat bread in her mouth and tore off a bite. She picked up her spoon and dunked it into her stew, her current foul mood not one that had ever usually taken ahold of her to this degree, only being spurned by one's mate hurt, badly.

"Are you all right?" Coll pressed his knee against her knee under the table as he spooned his own stew.

"Nay, I dinnae care for your continued denial, nor the attention you've always drawn from the maids, either now or in the past."

"The lass was only being polite."

"Aye, with her cleavage in your face and her coy promises of her willing hands. I noticed you didnae fix her neckline as you did mine." Another tearing bite of bannock.

"I didnae notice her cleavage." The scoundrel winked at Duncan, chuckled and continued to eat.

"Liar." Good grief. Give her a fork and she'd stick it in him.

Thankfully she didn't for what remained of their meal, instead allowing Duncan and Coll to chat on matters they'd yet to catch up on since Coll's return. A little guilt rolled through her for that. She'd taken him away from his duties when he must have so much to do. Aye, like prepare himself for his wedding.

Ugh. She finished her stew, thumped her spoon down and stood. "Please excuse me. I'm tired and wish to rest."

"Your chamber shall be the one right next to mine. Understood?" Coll scraped the bench back and rose to his full and towering height, the soft, faded brown leather of his pants molding his strong legs.

"Since you've made it clear that I'm no longer welcome at Carron, then you can hardly order me about by saying where I'll sleep." She couldn't help but issue that challenge. "No matter what you say, I'll sleep wherever I please."

"Ardan is the best place for you right now."

"So you say, and so I disagree." She shuffled around the table, kissed Ella and Duncan's cheeks and murmured a good night to them. A simpering lass she'd never be. With her cloak draped over her arm, she snatched up her satchel and basket and marched around the room toward the innkeeper where he stood speaking near the stairwell with a young maid of mayhap eight and ten and stopped next to him. "Excuse me, Gordon. There's been a change in plans regarding the third chamber the laird requested."

"That would be?"

"I'd like to sleep in the stables." The hay would make a soft bed.

"I cannae send ye out there, lass."

"Call me Fiona."

"The laird would have my head."

"Papa." The maid tucked a loose strand of her brown hair behind her ear. "Mistress Fiona can sleep in my room with me if she prefers."

Ahh, that would work too. She jumped on the maid's helpful offer. "Thank you. I'd like that."

"This is Mary, my eldest daughter." Gordon laid a gentle hand on the lass's shoulder. "Are ye certain, Mary?"

"Aye, Papa."

"Mary's room will be more than sufficient for my needs, and our laird will understand."

"Then Mary's room it shall be." Her answer seemed to satisfy him and he nodded at his daughter. "Ye make Mistress Fiona welcome in your room."

"Of course."

The innkeeper strode away and Mary plucked a candle from its holder on the wall and ducked into the shadowed nook under the stairwell. She opened a door. Wood creaked as she disappeared downstairs into the darkened depths. "This way," she called back.

"I'm coming." She followed Mary down the cramped stairwell, her shoulders brushing the gritty stone walls and the top of her head almost scraping the low beamed ceiling. Cool air swirled about and she dragged in a breath as her heartbeat raced. Never had she been all that overly fond of extremely tight spaces, and particularly not after being cornered by Jeremiah within just such a cramped stairwell a mere few days after Matthew's death at Rhue Castle.

Jeremiah had pushed her up against the wall late one night, his beady black eyes glinting in the candlelight flickering from an iron wall sconce. In her ear, he'd muttered, *"Now Matthew is gone, your care falls to me."*

"Please, let me pass." She'd tried to heave past him, only he'd shoved his hips against hers, his whiskey-laden breath washing over her and his lustful emotions dumping down hard.

"For years I've watched Coll's fascination for you grow. He followed your every move within my father's home. When you entered a room, I found myself doing so as well. You intrigue me. Why is it you married Matthew, a man castrated in his youth and still grieving deeply for his late wife? Surely he couldnae bring you any pleasure in the marriage bed without his cock to fill you up." Smirking, he'd gripped her breasts with his grubby hands, his fingers biting deep through the woolen cloth of her gown.

"Please, dinnae soil Matthew's good name in such a way."

"Could it be the empath in you couldnae refuse his needs?"

"You've no right to touch me like this, Jeremiah." She'd wanted to thrust her knee up and stab him in the groin, but without Matthew, her life lay in this man's hands and right now, she couldn't take the risk of angering Jeremiah any more than possible.

"I have no issue taking an unwilling lass, but with you I'd want more than just a rutting in a damp stairwell. I wish for a lover, and when I one day marry, for you to remain my leman. When I give you sons, they'll be bastards, but I'll see them want

for naught all the same, just as I will with you." He'd gripped her chin, his fingers and thumb digging in either side of her neck. *"Your door will always remain open to me, and only me. Am I understood?"*

"Are ye all right?" Peering up at her from the bottom step, Mary waited for her, the candlelight flickering across the damp stone walls, just as it had done that night six months ago at Rhue. This time though, no Jeremiah remained as a threat. She'd never return to his keep in the far north. Never.

"I simply have a dislike of confined spaces." She forced the memory away and stepped in beside Mary. "Show me your room, if you will."

"We are already here." Mary pushed open a door to the side of the stairwell, entered and touched her candle wick to the lamp on the wall next to the door.

She followed the lass inside and halted within a surprisingly large room.

Mary lit another couple of candles, one on each of the two side tables next to two basic wood-framed beds. The added light glowed over the stone walls and brushed the floorboards.

Mary heaved up the lid of an engraved wooden trunk in one corner, pulled out a sheet and flapped it over the unmade bed. She drew a white cotton case over a pillow and plumped it, then smoothed out a couple of thick brown furs over top.

"Thank you." She set her cloak, bag and basket at the end of the bed Mary had prepared, then at the side table, poured water from the jug into the basin. She washed her hands of the dust of her travels and splashed her face to refresh herself.

With a wide smile, Mary plopped down on her bed, pulled her knees to her chest and wrapped her arms around them. Rocking with a smile, she lifted her nose to the air and breathed deep. "Mmm, I can smell something very sweet within your basket."

"'Twas given to me by a friend and she said there are

goodies within, although I've yet to open it and see inside." Perhaps taking a look at what was within the basket might help distract her a little from her tumultuous thoughts.

She eased down onto the bed next to Mary and with the wicker basket on her lap, lifted the lid and gasped at the sight of a large tub of red strawberries. Although not strawberries she'd ever seen before. These were almost completely covered in something hard and brown, something suspiciously resembling mud. How strange.

"Oh, that is most unusual." Wide-eyed, Mary plucked one strawberry free by its stem and tapped the hard brown shell encasing the fruit. "Hmm, I wonder what this coating is."

"My friend has traveled far and wide, so it could be almost anything." She too plucked a fruit from the tub and examined it.

"Ships arrive often with all sorts of exotic wares from the lands far to the east of us. I adore riding to Carron Harbor to see them unload their vessels when they do."

"Then let's hope this is one of those exotic wares. Would you like to try a berry with me?"

"Aye, we'll see what this tastes like together." A firm nod from Mary, a sparkle of eagerness shining in her eyes. "On the count of three. One."

"Two." She tapped her berry against Mary's.

"Three." The lass popped hers in her mouth and so did she.

With a soft crunch, they both bit down.

Oh, sweet heaven. She moaned as the brown shell casing broke into pieces in her mouth and slowly melted against her tongue. The sweet flavor of the fruit blended deliciously with the full and rich elixir of the casing, the explosion of divine decadence making her sink back against the wall. Eyes closed, she savored the delight which had no name.

"I dinnae know what this mud is called," Mary mumbled around her mouthful from beside her, "but I'm so very glad you have a whole tub full of strawberries covered in it."

"Me too. Let's have another." She dove back into the tub then stopped as her fingers brushed a large block of something hard wrapped in shiny, purple parchment. She lifted the block out and gently slipped her finger under the top flap of the purple paper. The parchment fell away to uncover more of the same brown treat as what the strawberries were coated in, a large slab of it. "Well, well."

"Oh, how wonderful." Astonished, Mary clapped and jiggled on the bed. "What do the words on the parchment say?"

"Let me see." The largest word embedded upon the paper spelled something she'd never read before. She traced along it, murmured, "Choc-o-late."

"That must be the name for this treat." Mary jiggled some more. "Calling it mud seems so very wrong when it tastes naught like it. Choc-o-late. What a divine name."

"Here, we'll go halves with it." She broke the block in two and handed one half to Mary. "This is yours."

"Ye wish to share this treasure with me?" A powerful wave of delight rushed from the lass and nearly overwhelmed her.

"Aye." She laughed, even more delighted than Mary to have made her so very happy with such a simple gift. "This half is yours, and the other half is mine."

"Oh, I dinnae wish to eat all of my treasure at once." She scrambled to her feet, nabbed a clean cloth from the pile on the side table and wrapped her half of the chocolate within it, all except for one piece which she popped in her mouth and sucked away on madly. "This chocolate is sheer heaven."

"Fiona?" A knock rattled the door. "'Tis I, Ella. The innkeeper told me you wished to sleep downstairs in his daughter's room."

"I'm right here." She tucked her half of the chocolate bar back within the purple paper and slipped it into her satchel before rushing past Mary and opening the door. With one hand extended, she motioned Ella in. "Come, come."

"Speaking of my papa." Mary ferreted her chocolate away in her trunk and joined them. "I must go and aid him and Mama afore I can seek my rest. I'll be quiet when I return." She bobbed her head at her. "Dinnae fear that I shall wake you when I do."

"Thank you."

"Sleep well." Mary rushed upstairs, her steps echoing down the stairwell.

"Come see what Cherub packed within my basket. She brought me treats from her mate's twenty-first century time." During her visits to Ardan, she and Ella had spoken often of Cherub and how the fae princess had even intervened in her own chase with Duncan. Such a delight their fae guardian was. It had been wonderful to meet her.

"This I have to see, and during our trek to find you once you'd escaped Coll again in the meadow, he mentioned Cherub appeared to you in the woods." Ella dropped down onto the bed next to the basket, peered inside and frowned. "Is that mud covering these strawberries?"

"Nay, 'tis chocolate." She dropped in next to Ella, shuffled around and crossed her legs under her red velvet skirts. "Even though you've told me afore about Cherub, I still got quite the fright when she appeared out of the mist right afore me. Her skin sparkles as if dusted with diamonds."

"Aye, the eldest child born within the royal line always holds such sparkly skin. It denotes Cherub's strong lineage." Ella selected a strawberry and eyed her. "What did she speak to you about?"

"Just that she willnae allow Coll to set me aside a second time, and that I must continue to enforce the hunt until he sees reason. I even told Coll the same but he dismissed her words, said no bond existed. He fights it, even though 'tis clearly the truth."

With a thoughtful look, Ella twirled her strawberry by the stem in the center of her palm. The chocolate base encasing the fruit melted against her skin and left a glistening streak behind.

"Oh, it melts." Ella lifted her palm to her lips and licked the chocolate then eyes wide, gasped. "Oooh, this is sooo sweet." She popped the berry into her mouth and mumbled around it, "But let's no' forget the true matter at heart. When Coll finally sees reason and breaks his betrothal with the MacRae's daughter, the MacRae will never allow that kind of slight to pass."

"Aye, I am asking a lot of Coll." She could well be ensuring yet another war broke out.

"You are only asking him to accept your bond and deep inside his heart"—Ella stuffed another strawberry into her mouth—"he knows the truth, that you're his chosen one. It's just making certain he acknowledges it which seems to be the issue."

"His duty has always been to his clan, and to ensure his people's survival. What if I'm too late? He has given Elizabeth MacRae his word that they'll wed, and Coll never breaks his word once issued." Not in all the years she'd known him had he ever done so, which worried her terribly. With a shake of her head, she continued, "It goes against his very nature to put his own needs and desires above those of his clan, and that is exactly what I'm asking him to do in accepting our bond."

"Aye, but you're still his very heart and soul." Another strawberry and hearty moan. "He willnae be able to live without you."

"Yet he's lived without me for the past sixteen months and seemed to have no issue doing so."

"True, but there is also such deep devotion in his eyes when he looks at you." She grinned and winked. "Well, that and anger. Give him some time."

"I'm no' sure we have much time left."

The end of the week would be here within a matter of days.

Aye, she was nearly completely out of time.

Chapter 5

Coll stormed down the cramped stairwell after speaking to Gordon, the innkeeper. There wasn't a chance he'd allow Fiona to sleep below-stairs, not so far from his reach when she could so easily sneak out the front door and be gone before he knew it. And since she'd been so damn determined to ensure this chase, he didn't doubt she'd consider such an option.

"Calm down, Coll." Duncan gripped his shoulder from behind and halted him at the bottom of the stairs next to a flickering lamp. "I struggled to control my emotions too in the days afore I finally accepted my bond with Ella and took her as my wife. Your need to ensure Fiona's safety and wellbeing is all that will drive you until you claim her fully as yours."

"There isnae a bond, and I wish everyone would cease saying there is."

"Even I can see how greatly you desire her now that you're allowing your emotions their freedom. Trust me, the sooner you accept there is a bond and take her as yours, the far easier things will be for you both."

"I allowed her to wed Matthew, and no man who is soul bound to another would allow such a thing." He thumped his chest. "Now I cannae set Elizabeth MacRae aside for if I do, then

I may as well be declaring war with one of our allies. The safety of our clan comes first, no' my own needs and desires."

"Our seer, Hamish, said that part of the journey in finding our chosen one belongs in the chase. If you forego your bond with Fiona, then you'll regret it for the rest of your life. Dinnae make the same mistake I nearly did with Ella. At first I believed my only option was giving her up, both for her safety's sake and mine, but I was wrong, very wrong."

"Hamish didnae confirm or deny the bond existed."

The door whooshed open and Fiona stood there in her red velvet gown, her breasts pressed so deliciously tight against the white embroidered detailing at the edge of the low neckline. With her face pale and fingers twisted in her skirts, she cleared her throat. "I overhead your argument just now. Cherub confirmed our bond existed, even if Hamish didnae. Both Duncan and Ella believe we're mated, but it appears you're the only one who does no' wish to listen to any of us."

"If I wish to continue leading my clan then I must consider their needs first, no' my own." He couldn't lose the additional number of MacRae warriors who'd stand behind him in the current war raging across these Highlands. "I dinnae want you, Fiona, no' in any way."

"Liar." She shoved a finger in his chest. "But if that is what you wish to believe, then so be it." She stepped back into the room and returned with her black cloak donned and satchel in hand.

"Where are you going?" He seized her hand as she pushed past him, then almost drowned in the deep despair flaring in her beautiful blue eyes as she looked at him.

"I'm the one woman you'll never choose over any other. You walked away from me sixteen months ago, and now you're doing so again and stating your reasoning for why quite clearly. One day you will be the Chief of Clan MacKenzie, and I understand that you need Elizabeth MacRae at your side, so instead of continuing to argue with you, I'm simply going to congratulate you on your coming marriage and leave for Iona. I wish you both well, that you'll have a long life together and all of that."

"Dinnae you dare wish me well." He squeezed her fingers tighter.

"Leave me be." She snatched her hand back and eyed Duncan. "I wish to leave, to no longer remain near your hard-headed brother. Might I stay at Ardan House until I can arrange suitable passage to Iona?"

He heaved in front of his brother. "Like hell you're leaving right now. 'Tis late and I—I—" There wasn't a chance he'd allow his woman to retire to a damn nunnery. Fury blazed through him, so swift and sharp. Enraged, he scooped her up and stormed upstairs. He took the next flight two steps at a time then shoved the door of a chamber on the first floor—which he'd already been assigned—open and stomped inside. Knocking the door shut with his hip, he tossed her onto the fur-covered four-poster bed.

She bounced, her red locks flying all about her face. Thrusting her hair back, she slayed him with one very fiery look.

"No' a word," he warned. "You'll stay in my bed for the night, where I know you'll be safe and unable to leave. Riding through the dark when you've been traveling all day is dangerous. We're all exhausted and need to rest."

"You cannae tell me what I can or cannae—"

"And if you utter even one more word in argument, I'll bind and gag you."

"You will do no such thing."

"Dinnae push me, Fiona." He plucked her riding boots from her feet, dropped them on the floor then crawled in over top of her, his knees either side of her hips as he loosened the neck tie of her black cloak. "You'll also sleep on your side of this bed, while I sleep on mine. No more defying commands I issue. Am I understood?"

"There is no one more frustrating than you. That is what I understand."

"Good. I'm glad you've recognized that." He plucked the front laces of her bodice loose next, pushed her gown from her shoulders and tugged the long sleeves down her arms. He dragged the red velvet past her hips and down her legs, then in her white cotton shift, he rolled her under the covers. Never would he allow her to escape him again this night.

"I've never known you to be so forceful, Coll." She shivered, even though a fire had been lit and warmed the room.

"I'll hear no more complaints from you either." He tossed a large block of peat on the fire and the flames danced higher.

"And rude."

"No' another word." He heaved the heavy blue drapes across the window and stomped around to his side of the bed.

"I hate being soul bound to you." She thumped her pillow.

"I'm hardly a good catch. I agree." Boots toed off, he unfastened the ties of his brown leather pants while Fiona continued to glare at him. He shucked them and in only his tunic which thankfully reached him to mid-thigh, eased in under the covers and glared right back at her. Only his glaring didn't last long, not when the golden firelight flickered over the soft curves of her face and lit her tumbled curls into a blazing red hue. Damn it, how he wished to have her beside him each and every night to come, to be able to hold her in his arms and watch her as she fell asleep, to always know she'd be safe and close within his reach. His shoulders sagged, his defeat far too real. "Please, dinnae remain angry at me."

"Your stupid honor is unbending and completely annoying."

"A man's word, once given, cannae be taken back." His heart beat so sluggishly slow, the distance he'd instilled between them the greatest chasm. He wriggled a little closer.

"So I've noticed." She heaved over and gave him her back. "Finally I'm in bed with you, and all I hope for is to leave. Quite ironic really."

"I dinnae wish for you to remain angry with me." Gently, he reached out one hand and trailed his fingers through her hair. The silky mass of curls slid through his fingers and made him itch to touch more of her.

"Leave me be." She scampered closer to her edge.

"Go any farther and you'll fall out." This was the worst kind of torture, having her within touching distance and so angry at him. The kind of tortuous agony that sank bone-deep and twisted knife-hard.

A torture he'd brought upon himself.

Long minutes passed, each one bringing even more turmoil to his very soul.

"Coll?" She rolled back toward him, looked deep into his eyes. "Your pain is swamping me, like naught I've ever sensed afore. Why is your fae barrier down?"

"I didnae mean to drop it." He hauled it back into place. "Please forgive me, Fiona. I cannae part ways with you like this, and I need you to agree that you'll return to Ardan House with Duncan and Ella, and stay there. No catching passage on a vessel bound for Iona."

"I've no desire to remain anywhere near you and your future wife once you're wed. Are you truly going to speak vows with her? This is the last time I shall ask, and if your heart is truly set on her, then I'll say no more."

"Aye." He had no other choice. "She's the one I want to marry."

"Nay, she is the one you *need* to marry." She huffed a breath, her nose all wrinkled up. "Well, I guess that's it then. You're an ass, by the way."

"An ass who must think only of his clan. My people will always come first."

"I hate you." Tears glistened in her eyes. "And I hate your damn sense of honor too."

"It must be this way."

"Like I said. I willnae beg you to change your mind yet again. You've no more to fear from me." She wriggled back around and faced the fire, and his pain intensified.

He waited, until her breathing slowed and she finally succumbed to sleep and once she did, he drew her gently into his arms and held her tight. Only then could he breathe more easily.

Aye, this would be one of the longest, most tortuous nights of his life, and the coming days likely no better. Nose buried in her hair, he memorized her delicate scent, one that would forever torment him. White roses. Whenever he caught that fragrance again, he'd only ever think of her.

Chapter 6

A deep and sultry voice murmured words filled with wicked promises and nibbling kisses grazed her ear. Warm lips glided down her neck and—oh my. She opened one eye within the near dark of Coll's chamber, the embers in the fire all that remained aglow to light the room.

"Coll?"

"Mmm." He stroked the firm pad of his thumb over her shift-covered nipple, lowered his head to her breast and wrapped his lips—cloth and all—around the beaded tip. He sucked, hard, and her toes curled inward and dug into the mattress.

"What are you doing?" She sank her hands into his hair and arched her back. This couldn't be real. It had to be a dream considering how their last conversation had ended, unless of course he just wished for one more last tryst between the sheets, and knowing her, she'd gladly give into him just to have one more memory to keep.

He moaned against her breast, took the throbbing tip even deeper then released it with a soft pop before moving to her other breast and tracing that nipple just as he'd done the first.

"I believe we discussed our parting would soon occur, no' a possible bedding."

"Aye, we did, but I cannae keep my hands off you." He stroked one hand down her side, over her hip and along her outer thigh.

"I'll never agree to being your leman." Surely only heartache would follow if she did, only the sweet need currently racing through her very blood, and her deep desire to have at least this one last moment with him overrode all else. Aye, dawn had to be close and with the rising of the sun, so too would come their inevitable parting. One last touch. "What do you want from me, Coll?"

"I want your skin sliding against mine, and I want to touch you below, just as I did afore. I want to bring you pleasure and to make you come." The gold flecks in his brown eyes shimmered bright as he moved into a crouch between her spread legs and tugged her hem higher. "You're all I can think about. You consume my every thought, both day and night, always have and always will."

"Wait." She could barely breathe with how fast he moved. "You disrobe first."

"As you wish." With a wicked grin, he heaved his tunic over his head then let it slip slowly through his fingers until it pooled onto the covers beside them. His cock rose sure and strong from a nest of black curls, his large shaft saluting her high.

It beckoned for her touch and she gave into her own need and wrapped her fingers around him. He was so firm, thick and pulsing with life. A bead of his essence leaked free and shimmered on the head. Gently, she rolled her thumb over it. Aye, she wanted this moment, would never let it pass her by, no matter their parting would soon come.

Lifting up, she released him, but not for long. She smoothed her hands over his rigid pecs, the smattering of dark chest hair tickling her fingers. Oh, how she itched to touch all of him and greedy for more, she traced over his wide shoulders, caressed along the firm contours of his biceps and forearms then wriggled forward, swept her hands around to his back and over the curves of his tight buttocks. Her mate was allowing her to touch him. More, she needed more.

She cupped his balls in one hand, the fine hairs covering them silky smooth.

"What are you thinking, feeling?" His balls drew even tighter and higher, the hunger in his eyes blazing bright.

"I love you, Coll. I always have."

"Dinnae say that." He tipped her back, slid her shift up her body until he exposed her upper thighs then took her right foot in his hand and massaged the soft arch before trailing upward along her calf until he reached her knee. Smoothly, he set her foot down and massaged her other foot with the same firm, kneading touch. "I want to treasure this moment with you while I can, to never forget the sensation of your creamy skin under my fingers."

"I want to know your body as I know my own as well." She snuggled her head into her pillow, her anger at him from last eve flickering swiftly away.

"As I wish to know yours." He eased onto his belly between her legs, raised her knees over his shoulders and slid her shift higher, until his gaze caught on the red curls covering her entrance. With a deep inhale, he parted her folds and stroked along her sensitive slit. "There are simply no words to describe the emotions currently taking me, but my heart is pounding so hard, will likely heave from my chest soon enough. I hunger for a taste of you, to devour every inch of your flesh and to stamp my mark upon you."

"You may do as you please." Her heartbeat pounded fiercely too. She could never turn her chosen one away, not when their very souls were bound to each other's.

"I give you my word I willnae take your innocence." He pushed one finger inside her channel, stroked so decadently in and out before curving his finger into the perfect spot that had her rocking her hips for even more of his exquisite touch.

And more he gave her. He stroked higher and such pleasure ricocheted through her core, made her nipples stiffen into even harder points and abrade the soft cotton still covering them.

"I want to see all of you." Coll pushed her shift higher, past her belly and breasts then drew it over her head and dropped it on top of his tunic. Their clothing piled together looked so right, and as he cupped her breasts and plucked her nipples, the sight of him loving her even more so. "You're my fiery empath, always mine."

"I love how it feels when you touch me. Please, dinnae stop."

"I have no intention of stopping right now." He nibbled on her breasts, up the length of her neck, along her jaw then nuzzled in behind each of her earlobes. His teeth grazed her skin and she writhed against him, rolled her hips into his in a wanton way which she couldn't halt, the needy sensations spiraling through her in ever-increasing waves. "Are you ready for more?" he whispered raggedly in her ear.

"Aye," she panted, barely able to draw in a breath. "Although I fear I cannae take much more."

"You'll take everything I can give you." He pushed her legs wider with his legs, slithered down her body and nuzzled her mound until a feral sound rattled free from his throat.

"Are you all right?" She grasped his head, her fingers sliding into his midnight-black hair.

"Nay, my cock is about to break." He glided his fingers along her lower folds, dipped his head and kissed her right there, over her nub where all her pleasure stemmed from. "And you, my love, are a tasty wee treat I want to devour."

"Then devour away."

"Prepare yourself, for my hunger roars." He lapped at her nub, sucked it and flicked it with his tongue. 'Twas such divine torture, his rhythm deep and all-consuming as he brought her more pleasure than she could have ever imagined. Higher and higher, the sensations kept building and before she lost her mind and catapulted from the plateau he'd sent her climbing toward, she searched and found the hard length of his cock.

Pumping him in time with how he stroked one finger into her, she sought to bring him the same pleasure, and as his emotions flooded her, his fae-skilled barrier well and truly down, she held tightly onto each and every delicious feeling he offered her. "Kiss me, Coll. Please kiss me."

"I'm coming." He lifted himself up and over her, his warm, wet mouth connecting with hers as he continued to stroke her flesh below, his finger moving in a rhythm she completely adored.

"Coll." Her body cried out for his, to accept all of him. She craved him, his complete and full possession and right now she had nowhere to go but to soar from the edge of a cliff she wanted only to fly from. Such sweet pressure collided within her. "I cannae hold on any longer."

"Neither can I."

She wanted to make him come too, and as his cock swelled in her hand, she swiped across the head. He jerked and spurts of his hot seed gushed forth and coated her fingers.

"Ah hell." He buried his face in her neck as he continued to pulse in her fisted grip.

"Make me come with you."

"Aye, love, of course." He lifted up, looked deep into her eyes and flicked her clit. She broke apart, instantly splintered into a thousand different pieces, her core rippling with wave after wave of pure pleasure.

This was love.

This was the mated bond.

This was what he intended to deny them both of.

* * * *

Such intense sensations stormed through Coll as Fiona came around his finger, her body so responsive to his, and his to hers. She'd pumped his cock, given him such unexplainable pleasure and he'd shattered, even now still soared and had no desire to come back down.

"I need to feel you closer, Coll."

He needed to feel closer to her, too, had wanted to thrust deep inside her, to join them together in the ultimate way, only she wasn't his to take.

"Your emotions are still bombarding me." She caught his face in her hands and searched his gaze. "As long as you dinnae regret what we've just done, that is all that matters right now."

"I regret so many things, but touching you as I've done will never be one of them." He kissed her, wanted to do so much more but held back. "Do you still hate me?"

"Aye, with every inch of my body." She smiled, kissed the tip of his nose.

"You show it in strange ways." He kissed her cheeks then nipped her lower lip. "I want to see you come again. 'Tis most addictive watching you soar at my hand."

"You're a naughty man, yet I intend on being naughty too." Hands shoved to his chest, she pushed him onto his back, then crawled in over top of him and straddled his hips. Arms stretched high and her glorious mane of red hair swaying forward over her lush breasts, she wriggled against his groin, her slit rubbing along the base of his cock wedged firmly between them. "Oh, this feels sooo delicious. 'Tis the perfect way to awaken each morn."

"You're giving me the most wicked thoughts." With her breasts swaying heavy and full, he cupped them in his palms and longed to give them the attention they so deserved. "Lean forward. I want your tasty nipples in my mouth."

"I think no'." She squirmed back, her move denying him what he wanted as she positioned herself on her belly between his legs, her breasts resting softly either side of his inner thighs.

"What are you doing?"

"I'm about to make certain you never forget me, that I haunt your dreams for every night that is to come." She slid her hand around his cock, leaned forward and licked him from root to tip, her tongue swirling over the head and along his slit.

He groaned, all throaty and rough.

If his woman took him fully in her mouth and pleasured him in this way, he'd most definitely suffer a haunting in his dreams. "Are you certain you wish to do this?"

"I more than wish it." Peeking through her long sooty lashes tinged with red, she raised a brow. "Do you think me a wanton woman?"

"Aye, but you're my wanton woman, and I would have you no other way."

"Good." Her tongue slipped out again and after one long, mind-shattering lick of his shaft, she took his cock in her mouth, her rosy lips suctioning around him.

Gripping the sheets either side of him, he held on for dear life as she loved him with her mouth alone, her fingers caressing his balls, her touch so exquisitely soft and making them tighten and pull up. With her eyes closed, she bobbed up and down over him so wickedly. "Halt, please halt."

She sucked harder and oh hell, his mind went black with lust as she brought him to the brink of his control. Nay, he wouldn't seek his pleasure again until he'd swamped her in her own. Aye, when he soared into paradise, it would be with her.

Hands on her waist, he lifted her up and over his body then covered her mouth with his, the pressure of her lips sublime and the sensation of her tongue dueling with his beyond perfect. Her mouth had been made for kissing.

He drowned in the dark pool of desire she weaved around him, her soft curves molding to his body, her sweet femininity a perfect balance to his own harder angles. Then she gave even more of herself and overwhelmed his senses, her lips soft and coaxing one moment, then demanding and determined the next. He wanted to wake each morning with her kissing him in this exact way, to fit their bodies together as lovers did until rapture overtook them both.

Groaning, he drew her even more fully against him, the hard tips of her breasts rubbing against his chest and her hips rocking against his hips. He stroked down her back and over her bottom, until a fierce pressure built in his spine and sizzled around to the front. Closer. He needed to get even closer.

"Coll." She melted into him, their kiss intensifying, becoming more ravaging and insistent as she gave all of herself to him.

"I'm right here." He probed and plundered her mouth with each stroke of his tongue. Deeper, he moved, until his heart thundered a powerful beat against her heartbeat. Aye, only she could ever make him feel so complete with a simple kiss alone.

"Need to come." She rocked over top of him.

"Let go whenever you please. I'll be right here with you." Raw yearning took over and with a fierceness that demanded satisfaction, he angled his mouth more fully against hers, sank ever deeper into their kiss while she grasped his shoulders and moaned into his mouth.

Hands on her bottom, he spread her legs wider with his legs, until her lower folds rubbed against his cock wedged between them. Sliding her wet slit along his length without spearing himself inside her, he gave her all the pressure she needed, that he needed too. Hell, naught had ever felt so good. Sharp tingles speared up his shaft until he could no longer hold on.

"Now, Coll." Back arched and her breath hitching, she came and he exploded right along with her, his essence coating their bellies pressed together. She shuddered in his arms and he soared into heaven.

* * * *

Fiona floated in a daze as the last ebb of her pleasure faded away. Coll lay sated underneath her, an extremely satisfied grin on his face, one she'd put there and naught could have made her happier. "We should kiss more often," she whispered against his lips.

"I never knew kissing you could be so earth-shattering."

"Yet also messy earth-shattering." She rolled off him and slumped on her back at his side, pressed one hand to his seed smeared across her belly and giggled. "We need to bathe."

"I'll order the tub to be filled and a meal provided." He heaved out of bed and she wanted only to grab him and pull him back.

"You dinnae need to move so fast."

"If I dare stay in bed with you a moment longer, I'll be back to kissing you and ravaging you all over again."

"That sounds divine." She shuffled onto her side and grinned as he crouched naked before the remains of the fire, his biceps and back muscles rippling as he tore bark from a log and stuck the bits into the glowing embers. Blowing warm air onto the cinders, he worked the fire once more into roaring life and tossed a log over top. "You have a nice backside, my stubborn one."

"So do you, my fiery empath." With a mischievous wink, he sauntered across to the window and opened the blue drapes. Over his shoulder, the dawn sun hovered on the horizon and with those tight buttocks of his clenching even tighter, she admired the sweet view he offered.

She memorized the moment and softly sighed. Never would she forget this special time with him. "Could you bring me a wet cloth, please?"

"Of course." He strolled to the side table, dipped a cloth into the basin of water and cleaned his belly and cock before dunking the cloth again. He wrung it, drips splashing into the basin then sauntered toward her, the glint of desire in his eyes clear to see. "I'm going to wipe you clean."

"Nay, I intend to do that." She squirmed back.

"Wrong answer." He nabbed her ankles, pulled her back down the bed and spread her legs. With a wicked grin, he gently wiped her below then swept the cloth across her belly, which rumbled with hunger as he did.

"Ignore that."

"I'm done ignoring your needs, all of them, of which feeding you now comes first." Chuckling, he lobbed the cloth toward the basin where it landed with a splash then scooped up her bag and set it on the bed. He pulled out a clean shift and tugged it over her head.

"Aye, well, I am most certainly famished, wouldnae mind finding my basket which I left behind in Mary's room. There are treats aplenty within it."

"I'll go and fetch it after I gather us a tray from one of the maids." He pulled on a clean white tunic and donned his great plaid at his waist, laced his boots, strapped his weapons in place and strode to the door, his black hair mussed and dark stubble shadowing his jaw. "I'll ensure hot water is ordered for our bath. Dinnae move, no' an inch. I shall no' be long."

"Now I truly do feel like a wicked wench awaiting the return of her lover."

"You are more than my lover, Fiona."

"Aye, I'm a dear friend too." An admission she'd dearly love to forget he'd mentioned.

"Stay here." A murmured answer as the door clicked shut behind him, his footsteps drifting away down the passageway.

Under her breath, she whispered back, "You're far more than my lover, Coll MacKenzie. You are my mate, whether you wish to admit it or no'."

Beyond the window, the thundering of horses' hooves pounded toward her and she snuck out of bed and tiptoed to the sill. Pushing the window wide, she leaned over the edge. Below in the tavern's inner courtyard surrounded by leafy elm trees, a score of riders galloped in and hauled their mounts to a stop near the stables.

The warrior at their party's head leaped from his war horse, his brown beard flecked with gray and his unmistakable MacRae plaid fastened around his waist and hooked over one shoulder. A thick brown leather vest flapped loose over his tunic. She'd seen him once before, when he'd visited Duncan and Ella at Ardan House during one of her own visits there two months past. The emblem engraved on the pin of his plaid at his waist held the MacRae clan chief's arms. He was the Chief of MacRae, John MacRae. One of his sons had even wed a lass from the fae village and she'd given birth to a child who held an intensely strong fae ability, that of the "power of thought." The MacRae's son had brought his wife and child to Ardan to see the seer and his sister, to ensure the young lad received the necessary training in his burgeoning skill. She'd even witnessed what the lad could do.

John MacRae strode toward a young woman mounted on the horse behind him. The lass's rich auburn hair, so similar in color to her own red locks, fluttered down her back. She must be Elizabeth, although this lass she'd never met.

In an emerald woolen riding habit, she smiled at her chief. "Why must we stop now, Father? We're almost at Carron Castle. I wish to see my betrothed."

"I'll send a rider ahead and inform Coll of our coming arrival. We're expected, although you might like to freshen up first afore we complete the last leg of our journey. We'll partake of a meal and continue on once we have." He hoisted the lass down from atop her horse and she kissed her father's cheek affectionately, her love for him clear to see in her eyes.

Soon that love would be gifted to her mate, and that realization sank in bone deep and heart-wrenchingly hard.

The young woman pulled her brown fur cloak tighter about her to ward off the chilly morning air, her nose and cheeks glowing a healthy shade of pink and her breath puffing in a fog from her mouth.

The last thing she wished to do was witness the lass fawning over Coll when she discovered him downstairs. She pulled the drapes closed, her chest so heavy and her very soul tearing in two. Mayhap she shouldn't have allowed Coll's touch this morn, only he'd been impossible to turn away from, and the memories from their time together would be ones she'd always treasure.

Aye, her future was once again set, and unfortunately it still wasn't with Coll. The Isle of Iona beckoned, as well as the high walls of the abbey where she'd seek refuge and mayhap eventually find some healing for her own heart.

She unfolded her royal blue gown from her satchel and shimmied the soft velvet over her head then with the long sleeves draping over her wrists, added her favorite golden tasseled girdle before lacing her riding boots on. With her red gown gifted from Coll tucked safely away in her bag, she fastened her fur-lined black cloak over her shoulders and with all her belongings in hand, opened the door.

Carefully, she checked each direction of the passageway, the doors leading off each side closed and only the small window at the end of the hallway allowing light to filter through. All remained clear. She snuck downstairs, ducked into the darkened alcove under the stairwell and peeked into the main room.

The MacRae's warriors, a good score of them, had all entered and taken seats at the tables, while Mary and another two serving maids weaved around the men and passed them bowls of steaming oats and tankards of ale. She searched amongst the warriors and found Coll standing near the fireplace with Elizabeth and her father. His biceps bulged as he slid one thumb under his sword's leather strap at his waist, the hilt of his blade gleaming.

"We didnae expect to find you here rather than at your keep." Elizabeth batted her long lashes at him, which made her belly heave with distaste.

"I didnae expect to see you here either. Come and sit. We'll break our fast together." With one sweeping gesture, Coll motioned for Elizabeth and her father to sit and the three of them took their places at a table.

Aye, Coll now wished to break his fast with his betrothed rather than with her. She slid back out of sight into the nook, tears welling in her eyes and blinding her.

He'd told her countless times that he believed no bond existed between them.

For him it clearly didn't, even though it did for her.

Their bond would be one that now never saw completion.

She dragged in a stuttered breath.

She'd promised him she wouldn't beg him to change his mind yet again. He had no more to fear from her.

'Twas time to leave.

* * * *

Coll gritted his teeth as he sat next to Elizabeth. All he wanted to do was stride back upstairs and claim his—he shook his head. Ah hell. Who was he kidding? Fiona was far more than a dear friend, and his time with her this morn had proven that to him beyond a doubt. She was his, just as he was hers. Never could he lie with this woman seated beside him. Making love with Elizabeth made him shudder with disgust.

His heart and soul belonged to the girl who'd once sat upon a ledge under a waterfall with him, their feet dangling into the pool and the sunlight playing through the sheet of water and sending pretty beams of light shimmering over her. She'd been the only one to consume his every thought since, and no matter he'd ridden away from her sixteen months ago and allowed her to wed Matthew, he'd only done so knowing theirs would be a marriage in name only.

Aye, over the years, he'd lived and breathed for her, and for the past two days, he'd been chasing her across the Highlands because she held the other half of his soul and he could be nowhere else but with her. Cherub had even appeared before her, decreed they were soul bound, and the seer, Hamish, had all but said the same as well in the words he'd imparted to Ella of his vision. How much more evidence did he need? It was only his thick head and unbending honor getting in his way from accepting his true future. One with Fiona, his soul bound mate and chosen one.

He couldn't lose her again, not even for the sake of his own clan. Aye, he'd certainly do all he could once he'd broken his betrothal with Elizabeth to mend the discord he'd soon cause between him and the MacRae, but the chief of their allied clan had always had a fairly reasonable head on his shoulders. The man's son had even wed a lass of fae blood, and his wee grandson had recently come into his own fae skill, that of the "power of thought." The MacRae understood soul bonds, and hopefully he'd understand that one had formed between him and Fiona as well.

"What brought you to this inn?" Elizabeth cleared her throat from beside him, her cheeks flushed as she pressed a hand to her chest. "My apologies. I dinnae mean to pry, but we surely didnae expect to find you here."

"An errand." He accepted a bowl of oats from the maid and thanked her.

"That errand is now done?" She smiled so prettily and he tried heartedly hard not to scowl.

'Nay, that errand will fill my days and nights for what I hope is the rest of my life." As soon as he'd spoken to John MacRae, he'd find Fiona, get down on one knee and apologize to her profusely. He'd do whatever it took to gain her forgiveness, because he surely couldn't live without her a moment longer.

"Pardon?" Eyes wide, Elizabeth frowned at him.

He had a great deal of apologizing to do, to this lass as well. He opened his mouth to speak, then closed it again. It would pay for him to have this conversation with her father first.

"My daughter," the MacRae said from across the table with his brows drawn together in deep lines, "will make you a fine wife, Coll. Strengthening the allied bonds between our clans is essential."

"I agree, John. We need to strengthen our allied bonds, but we may need to look at *other* ways in which we might do so."

"What *other* ways are you speaking of?" The MacRae slammed his palms down on the table and rattled the legs.

"I hope I'm no' imposing." Ella stepped in beside him, her cream shirt tucked into her black breeches and her brown hair pulled back into a braid and secured with a lacy ribbon. She squeezed his shoulder. "I caught sight of the MacRae's party arriving from my chamber window. Duncan will join us in but a moment."

"Ella, meet Elizabeth and her father, John MacRae." He motioned to them. "This is Ella, my brother's wife and a fae compeller from the Matheson village."

"'Tis lovely to meet you." Elizabeth beamed wide and laid her hand daintily on his arm as she answered Ella. "My brother's wife is from your village too, and their wee son has recently come into his skill, that of the 'power of thought.'"

"Duncan has spoken of the lad." Ella nodded at her. "Although I've only recently arrived at Ardan myself and missed meeting your kin while they stayed there during the time the boy trained with our seer and his sister."

"Speaking of the fae." Coll shoved to his feet, startled Elizabeth as he did but without time to apologize, he grasped Ella's hand. "I need a favor. Could you go and sit with Fiona, our fae empath, while I speak to John. It appears Cherub was right, and now I'm well aware of it. Dinnae let her out of your sight. She's in my chamber."

"Of course."

"Thank you, and tell her I willnae be long."

"I certainly shall." Smiling wide, Ella pranced out of the main room and fairly skipped up the stairs.

"You have a woman called Fiona in your chamber?" With a rumbling growl, John stood, the white lines around his mouth pinching tight as he narrowed his gaze. "Explain yourself, Coll."

"For this coming conversation, we need to speak in private." He gestured toward the passageway. "The innkeeper keeps a private antechamber available for those who need to use it down the hallway."

"Lead the way." Gritting his teeth, John motioned to one of his warriors to remain with his daughter and the beefy guardsman took a standing position behind the lass.

This coming conversation was one that needed to occur, and with all haste. Coll strode from the room with the MacRae and entered the private room he'd used a number of times. He closed the door after John had walked through then waited as the man sat in the upholstered burgundy chair beside the window overlooking the hills.

He eased into the blue padded seat opposite John, planted his elbows on his knees and pressed his hands together.

"In what *other* ways are we to strengthen our allied bond, other than by marriage as we've already arranged?" John gripped the hilt of his side sword, the fierce warrior well known for his fast and lethal strike with his blade. "And why the hell would you speak of another lass being within your chamber right in front of my daughter? Do you have no care for Elizabeth's feelings at all?"

"I apologize, but I can no longer marry your daughter." No mincing of words. "'Twould be gravely unfair to wed her when I'm in love with another woman."

"I beg your pardon?" John slid his claymore free, his voice

all raspy and hard as he shoved to his feet. "Surely I just misheard you."

"I'm no' free to wed Elizabeth, no when I've given my heart to another." Rising to his feet too, he swung his own sword free. "The fae empath, Fiona, holds the other half of my soul, as I hold the other half of hers."

"Damn you, Coll." Nostrils flaring, MacRae loosened his knees and took a ready position. "My daughter will face ridicule and scorn when word spreads of your decision to toss her aside in favor of another woman, no matter that woman is your mate."

"I can offer recompense for the broken betrothal. Name your price and it shall be paid." He too inched from side to side, his gaze on MacRae as he awaited his strike which would surely come.

"My daughter's very reputation is at stake. I should kill you, right here and right now for the slur you've now brought down upon her name." John swung and Coll blocked his swift blow. Their swords clashed dead center and clanged loud.

Aye, this battle of retribution was inevitable, but he'd fight to his last breath to ensure he had the chance to claim Fiona as his wife. He wanted her by his side for the rest of his life, and he damn well wished he'd seen the truth sooner. "I willnae lay my blade down. We shall fight if you wish it. I leave the choice to you."

"Aye, we fight." John shoved forward and shoulder to his chest, flattened him to the wall behind him. The wall hangings swayed and sparks flared from the brazier. "I demand suitable retribution, in the form of your blood."

"Until first blood is drawn then." He heaved John from him then ducked the warrior's next blow aimed at his neck. "I see you dinnae wish to hold back on this fight."

"My daughter is an innocent."

"As is Fiona, her welfare and safety mine to ensure." He thrust his knee into MacRae's groin, bore his shoulder into him and took him down to the floor, both their swords clattering across the ground. "Have you ever loved afore, John? So greatly that you would surely die if you couldnae hold your loved one close?"

"Of course." John pushed and rolled them both. The warrior came up over top of him and gripped his shirtfront. "She's my only daughter, Coll, and you'll break her heart with this news."

"Excuse me, but I could hear the disturbance you two are causing from the main room, and now there are warriors aplenty ready to tear in here." Duncan shut the paneled door behind him and eyed John. "Your son's wife is of fae blood, just as you're aware Coll and I are, and now my brother has discovered a soul bond has formed between him and Fiona, or at least I take it he's finally admitted that truth to you since you're now both battling."

"Aye, he's admitted the truth." A grunt from John.

"He loves her," Duncan continued, "wishes to claim her, but cannae do so until he is freed from his agreement to wed your daughter. I want for my brother what you'll one day want for your grandson, for him to find his chosen one and join with her in all ways. You must release Coll from his agreement and allow us to find another way to deepen our allied bonds. We'll find a way that suits us all."

"Only a touch of fae blood has ever entered my MacRae line." John heaved to his feet, gripped Coll's lapels and hauled him up too. "You're truly mated to this Fiona you've spoken about?"

"Aye, and ''tis a bond I cannae relinquish. I've spent days trying to deny it exists, but no more can I do so. I love her."

"Then you're one damn lucky bastard for being mated to another of fae blood."

That he now understood, to the depths of his heart. "What of Elizabeth? I have feared hurting her."

"I'll need to consider her options and act swiftly. In the

meantime, you'll need to keep any knowledge of your relationship with your mate quiet for as long as you possibly can. Be aware though that I intend on spreading the word that 'twas Elizabeth who has chosen to turn you down after a disagreement arose between you." MacRae blew out a long breath as he scooped his sword and sheathed it. "I'll procure her another betrothal during that time, and afterward we shall all speak again on what *other* ways we might strengthen our alliance. You owe me a great deal, Coll."

"I do, and I'll make amends." He nabbed his own sword and belted it. "That I promise you."

"Coll!" Breathing hard, Ella rushed in. "I cannae find Fiona. She wasnae in your chamber and I've also checked the stables. The stable hand said she left no' long after John and his party arrived. She's riding toward the coastline, gave the lad implicit instructions that you were to collect your horse at the harbor village. The lad said she wished to secure passage to the abbey on Iona."

"I'll never be able to get her back if she makes it to the abbey. We ride now." He raced out the door and left John behind, Duncan and Ella hot on his heels as he sprinted across the yard toward the stables. He grabbed Duncan's war horse and heaved into the saddle, while his brother mounted Ella's steed and hoisted his wife up in front of him.

Leather creaked and he galloped across the rolling moors toward the western coastline.

Duncan pounded in beside him, Ella secured safely in front. "Fiona loves you," his brother yelled over the wind, "would never truly stand in your way when your desire is foremost to ensure the safety of our clan. That's why she's left. I'd all but guarantee it."

"I never acknowledged our bond existed to her, although I had intended on doing so after I'd spoken to John." He gripped Duncan's arm as they rode, then just as quickly released it. "You have my immense thanks for what you said to John just afore."

"John's daughter-in-law and grandson are of fae blood. He clearly understands far more about the mated bond than you thought to give him credit for." Duncan leaned in closer to his mount's neck, cocooning Ella more tightly to his chest. "We need to catch Fiona now, and you need to make amends, immediately."

"Agreed." Once he caught up with her and apologized profusely, he intended on spending every day of the rest of his life attempting to make up for the grave mistake he'd made in ever letting her go. She was the only one he'd ever love, ever wished to live for.

"Look!" Ella pointed to the trail up ahead where it veered into two, this road one that many travelers used with it being so close to Carron Harbor. "Your destrier has a heavier track mark on its front right hoof and your horse has veered away."

He caught the clear impression too. His horse no longer being ridden toward the harbor but into the forest rising alongside the inner channel of the loch. She'd changed course. He shoved his knees into his destrier's flanks and spurred his horse on. "I'm coming, my fiery one," he whispered raggedly, his very soul crying out to hers. "I'm coming, and never will I let you go again."

Chapter 7

An early evening mist clung to the shrub-lined trail as Fiona galloped through the woods toward Carron Castle. When she'd ridden from the tavern it had been with the intention of seeking passage on a vessel headed toward Iona, yet when the harbor had come into view, fear had struck her hard. Never could she live without Coll, or even attempt to do so, and even though he'd be furious about her return to his keep, she intended on making one final stand. Or at least she would once his anger had calmed.

Fallen leaves twirled along the pathway as she raced and a bone-deep chill invaded her body, making her shiver from the cold. No longer did the sun shine as it had this morn, but instead gray clouds obscured the skies high above. She wriggled in her saddle and tried to stretch tired muscles after the long hours of riding.

Onward, she raced, his war horse solid and powerful underneath her, until she finally emerged from the forested trail and pulled the beast to a halt. Carron Castle rose tall and strong along the cliffs overlooking the innermost point of Loch Carron, the sight so incredibly welcoming.

This was the place where she'd sought sanctuary after escaping Rhue Castle and Jeremiah, and this was the place where she wished to spend the rest of her life, and with the one man she loved more than anyone else.

She slapped her reins against the horse's neck and spurred the beast on.

The head guardsman caught sight of her and she waved out and galloped under the main arch then drew her horse in as she reached the front step of the keep within the inner bailey.

She slung one leg over the side, dropped to the ground and tossed the reins to a lad who rushed forward. "Ensure our laird's horse is well fed and brushed down."

"Aye, mistress." The lad led the horse away.

"And where would our laird be?" Kyla stood on the top step under the eaves in a burgundy gown, her hands braced on her hips and her golden-red curls lifting in the light wind.

"'Tis a very long story, but we are in fact mated and I cannae yet allow him to get away from me simply because he continues to deny our bond exists." With her satchel slung over one shoulder, she walked across to her dearest friend and hugged her. "He still intends on speaking vows with Elizabeth, and I intend on confronting him again, although only once he's calmed down. He'll be beyond angry that I'm here when expects me to stay at Ardan."

"He still intends to wed the MacRae's daughter even though you are soul bound?" A disbelieving look flared in Kyla's eyes, quickly followed by fury, the wave of emotion rolling from her matching her expression. "Cherub arrived here and I sent her to you, but you can be certain I'll have a stern word with Coll as well when he returns. How can he continue to ignore the truth right afore his very eyes?"

"I've no idea, but I intend to make certain he no longer—"

"The laird returns!" The guardsman's call echoed toward her and her heart almost catapulted from her chest.

Damn it. Coll should never have been able to follow her this fast, not when he had his bride-to-be to care for, only horses' hooves indeed pounded then as two mounts hurtled under the arch, dust swirled into the drizzly mist. Nay, she needed more time to consider how to approach their next argument, for there surely would be one.

Coll bounded from his mount in thick black boots, his plaid belted around his waist and sword swaying at his side, a determined and fierce slash crossing his face. His black hair blazed blue on the ends, his locks disheveled and his piercing brown eyes flecked with gold landing right on her. "Fiona MacKenzie, you and I are about to have words."

"I've got to go." She dashed past Kyla and raced up the stairs to her chamber on the top floor.

"Halt!" Coll bellowed as he pounded after her, his booted steps ricocheting off the walls.

She skidded inside her chamber and slammed the bolt across.

"Open this door now!" Coll hammered and rattled the door.

"I dinnae want you anywhere near me until you've calmed down."

All went suddenly quiet on the other side and she pressed her ear to the door.

"You'll never bar me from your chamber again." His voice rumbled from behind her and she spun around, her belly dropping to her feet as Coll shut the connecting door between their rooms and strode toward her.

"Wait." She lifted her hands.

"Running from me isnae acceptable." He stopped in front of her, unfastened his sword belt and set it aside, kicked off his boots and heaved his white tunic over his head. In naught but his kilt, the front tenting something wicked, he murmured, "I love you."

"Pardon?"

"I said, I love you, infuriatingly so." He pressed her back against the door then with his hands planted on the paneled wood either side of her head, he leaned in and touched his forehead to hers. In the softest whisper, he murmured, "I've broken my betrothal agreement and right now I intend on speaking handfast vows with you. Will you do me the great honor of marrying me, my fiery empath?"

"What?" She swayed and he pressed his body firmer against hers, his cock jabbing through his plaid and stabbing into her belly.

"None can ever learn of our relationship outside of this keep, no' until after John has secured another betrothal for his daughter, but he shall do so quickly. I've no doubt about that."

"I—I—"

"John's agreed we'll speak again and discuss other ways of strengthening our allied bonds."

"But—"

"I'll begin with our vows."

"Wait." Shock swarmed through her. "I love you too."

"I want a full joining, to complete our bond in every way, and I want it now."

"You truly believe there's now a bond?" For so long he'd denied it, and she needed to hear him say he believed her one more time.

"I believe you. There is a bond, and I promise to apologize every day for ever disagreeing with you, as well as to find interesting ways in which to make those apologies." He pushed her cloak from her shoulders, unlaced her bodice's front stays and tugged the blue velvet of her sleeves down her arms. Then with a quick pull at her waist, the fabric whooshed to her feet.

She stood in naught but her shift, and never had anything ever felt so right. "I must be dreaming."

"There'll be no more dreaming for either of us. This is real, and neither shall we be leaving these chambers until I've ravaged you senseless."

"That hardly sounded like a threat if that was your

intention."

"'Tis time for that ravaging to begin, right now." With painstaking slowness, he grazed one finger from between her breasts to her belly, his sensual touch making her blood heat and a heady warmth flutter to life in her core.

"I really love how you touch me, Coll."

"I'm going to come inside you this time." He skimmed his hands over her waist and around to her bottom, lifted her up and carried her into his own chamber where he laid her down on the soft fur bedcovers and slid in over top of her. Gently, he pressed his mouth to her lips. "Do you agree?"

"Aye, I agree."

"Good." He picked up one side of the bedsheet, tore a strip from it, clasped his right hand with her right, and wrapped the white cotton around both their wrists. With them bound together, he touched his lips to hers again. "I, Coll Duff MacKenzie, of Carron Castle, pledge my troth to Fiona MacKenzie. With this handfast, I take her as my wife for the next year and a day, and as the woman who holds my soul for all time to come." He threaded his fingers firmly through hers. "The moment I can procure a clergyman to oversee our formal marriage vows, I shall."

"I cannae believe this is happening."

"Believe it." He hoisted her shift up and settled it over her belly as he spread her legs.

"Oh, you're so close." More heat flooded her below, her hunger for him rising so swift and strong. "I, Fiona MacKenzie, of Carron Castle, pledge my troth to Coll Duff MacKenzie. With this handfast, I take him as my husband for the next year and a day, and as the man who holds the other half of my soul for all time to come."

"Perfect." Grinning, he striped his kilt away, rocked his hips against her hips, his cock pushing against her entrance and his gaze heating to a smoldering hue, "Are you ready to seal our vows with a kiss?"

"I'm ready to seal them in whatever way you desire."

"You're my wife, now, always, and forever." He lowered his mouth to hers and took her lips in a searing kiss, one that completely muddled her mind.

"Come inside me."

"Soon. First I intend on preparing you. I've no wish to hurt you and I am no' a small man, in case you missed that." He pulled the binding free of their wrists, eased her shift fully over her head, tossed it aside and drifted down her body.

She grasped his broad shoulders and caressed his biceps as he devoured her breasts, his cock rubbing along the inside of her legs and making her weep for him below. Her stomach tightened in eager expectation, her heartbeat pounding and her body crying out for a full claiming.

Aye, she craved his touch, all of his touch. Her chosen one was a man who'd never been far from her during her youth, and now she intended on keeping him close every day to come. Their mated bond was one they might have set aside until now, but no more. Every hard and defined inch of him was hers to treasure and adore, and she would, for all time to come. "Let me touch you, Coll."

"Later. 'Tis my time to touch you first." He dipped his fingers between them and grazed along the inside of her thighs then gently, swept his hand along her slick entrance, his touch an intimate caress which would always belong to her. Then as he dipped one finger inside her and stroked deep, she arched her back and demanded more.

"Claim me, as those who are soul bound do." She caught his face in her hands, gazed into the glorious depths of his heavenly eyes. "Complete our bond and make me yours in every way."

"That, I cannae wait to do." He added a second finger and pushed ever deeper inside her, until exquisite pleasure radiated out and she moaned her approval.

So sublime.

"I'm ready, right now." Beyond ready

* * * *

Greedy for the same completion of their bond, Coll rose up and gripped Fiona's hips, then slowly and carefully, he teased his cock along her slick folds. "Open wider for me, my love."

She spread her legs wider. "I know they'll be a little pain, but I'm ready for it."

"Hopefully the pain willnae last for long." Covering her mouth with his, he kissed her and attempted to distract her mind. He licked across her tongue and as he did, he pushed against her thin barrier below and unable to hold back a moment longer, tore through her innocence in one fast thrust.

"Oh goodness," she gasped against his lips.

"Are you all right?"

"Aye." She held onto him piercingly tight, her legs wrapped around the backs of his legs, her fingers digging into his biceps and her body trembling. "You're definitely a big man, but glad I am you fit."

"I'll take this slowly." He pulled back, until he nearly came out of her, then joy rushed through him and he sank ever-so-slowly back inside her. "Tell me what you like and what you dinnae like."

"I feel so at peace, yet also hungry for even more. I want you to go faster." She clutched his butt and urged him to move. "We're one, and never shall we be parted again."

"Aye, my hunt for you is now done. I've captured you and made you mine. Never will you get away from me again." With one hand on the mattress, he eased up then slid with tortuous slowness back in again. He repeated the move, over and over again, until a sizzling pressure built in his balls and fired up his shaft.

"Oh, sooo perfect. Go faster." She moaned her pleasure and

he increased his pace, his thoughts consumed by his woman, his mate. He pounded harder and deeper inside of her, each of his claiming strokes met by her as she lifted her body to his. "Coll, I cannae hold on any longer."

"Neither can I. Let go, my fiery empath. I'm right here with you." Driving deep, he reached down between then and caressed her nub and as he did, she screamed, her inner muscles clenching down on him and locking him in place. He bucked into her, her greedy channel sucking at him and his essence spurting from him and coating her deep within.

Aye, together, they soared to the heavens and never had such peace assailed him. This was the moment he'd been waiting for, to join as one with the woman he'd always desired. If only he'd recognized it sooner.

"Dinnae leave me again, Coll." With a soft sigh, her lashes fluttered down.

"Never again. That I can assure you." He rolled onto his side and tucked her safely within his arms, while outside the window the sky darkened and the moon and stars came out to play. He'd finally made her his, the woman he'd adored his entire life, the lass who'd never allowed him to give up on the hunt.

Aye, this was his woman, the only one he'd ever crave, ever love, ever adore with all his heart and soul.

* * * *

Fiona lay still as she floated amongst the stars. This was heaven having her chosen one lying beside her and holding her so deliciously tight. With firm possession, he palmed one of her breasts, his thumb swiping over her nipple and making it stiffen further.

"Open your eyes, love. Look at me." He licked around her nipples, first one and then the other before sucking one nipple deep inside his mouth and playing the tip with his tongue.

Sweet heat rose once more within her core and radiated

outward, made her thrust her breasts ever deeper into his exquisite touch and whimper his name. "Coll."

"I've got you." He caressed down her body and rubbed her nub as he continued to lave her breasts and she moaned as white-hot pleasure rippled through her, so swift and fast. She soared again as he drove her over the edge, her body so in harmony with his touch and even more stars sizzled to life amongst the myriad already ablaze until slowly, ever so slowly, she came back down.

Coll grinned at her. "That was beautiful to watch." He leaned in, nibbled on her lobe, the promise in his eyes all she'd ever hoped to see. "I may be insatiable for a while. I want to see you coming at my hand, over and over, until you cannae breathe for the pleasure."

"I shall have no complaints in that regard." Such happiness thrummed through her, her chosen one's acceptance of their bond the most magical gift she could've ever wished for, their mated bond so strong and the most enchanting of all. "But I believe 'tis now my turn to bring you pleasure. I wish to see how else we might join together as one."

"There is only one way at present." His happiness flared from him and smothered her in its exquisite hold, then he rolled her smoothly underneath him again, aligned every inch of their bodies and with his shaft swelling and lengthening, slid his cock deep inside her in one fast lunge.

"Oh my." Back arched, the sheer rightness of having him within her overtook her emotions.

"Is all well?" He caressed her bottom and rocked his hips against hers and as he did, she stroked his sculpted chest and skated along the enticing path of his glorious abs. Golden sparks burned in his stunning brown eyes flecked with gold.

"Very well, my stubborn one."

"I apologize for taking so long in admitting our bond existed." He dipped his head and kissed her, his tongue sweeping across hers in a delicious and languorous caress, one she'd crave until the end of her days.

"You feared acknowledging our bond, and I understand why." Her body clenched down on him, so tight and he groaned, thrust balls-deep inside her and she was lost.

The impact of their fast joining sent her spiraling back into the heavens and she floated as he joined her in another realm, one far beyond their own.

Aye, they'd completed their bond and her chosen one had now claimed her in every way.

Never would she need to run from him again.

He was hers.

Her lover.

Her every wish and desire.

Her every dream come true.

Chapter 8

The next night, Fiona lay slumped across Coll's chest within his royal blue canopied bed, the heat from the fireplace washing over her. They'd spent an entire day in bed and naught more could she have asked for, his attention dedicated to her and now saturated in bliss, she skimmed her fingers across his muscled torso. "I'm hungry."

"I just fed you." He'd accepted a dinner tray when the maid had knocked and he motioned to the remnants of their evening meal on the side table. They'd enjoyed succulent goose and roasted vegetables, food they'd hand-fed each other right before making love all over again.

"This time I mean for chocolate. I never did get the chance to share the contents of Cherub's basket with you, but I did snag half a chocolate bar which should still be in my satchel. You must try it." Grinning, she pushed up and scooped her bag from beside the bed where she'd set it a few hours ago with the intention of showing him the treat, only he'd sidetracked her with his kisses and she'd forgotten all about it. Flap open, she rummaged within and found the treasure she sought.

"What is this chocolate you speak of?" He gripped her hips, toppled her back onto the thick fur blankets beside him, the chocolate bar now thankfully in her hands.

"Try this and discover the decadent taste for yourself." She broke off a piece, set it on top of her nipple and grinned as the sweet treat melted against her skin and slid down into the valley between her breasts.

"That is an offer I will never decline, not with how you're currently serving it up." He swept his hands down her body and caressed her bare bottom. He lifted her higher and suctioned his mouth around her chocolate-coated nipple. Groaning, he sucked and as she placed another piece of chocolate on her other nipple, he licked across to it and moaned some more.

Imbibing, he devoured her and when she smoothed a piece along her lips, he surged upward and with breathless hunger, kissed her before she abandoned the rest of the chocolate block and entwined her body fully with his.

Love each other they would, for the rest of their lives.

Aye, no one would ever separate them again.

It was time for her to revel in her Highlander's touch.

And most certainly, 'twas time for the fae to live.

Chapter 9

Atop the ramparts of Carron Castle, Cherub stood hand-in-hand with Kirk, her cloaking extended over them both as they remained unseen to one and all. As the midnight moon shone high overhead, its golden rays swept across the land and bathed it in a rich, shimmery hue. "This night marks such a wonderful new beginning for Coll's clan."

"It surely does." Kirk pressed her back against the stony wall next to the crenellation, his solid body warming her through. "Coll and Fiona have spoken handfast vows, and their bond now well and truly completed. Where to next, my elusive imp? I can't wait to undertake our next adventure."

"Neither can I. Give me a moment." The breeze rose, the air swirling and whispering across her skin and along with it bringing all the secrets it held, including a glimmer of need from far in the future, from Kirk's own twenty-first century time. "I can sense a great need from within Murdock Matheson's clan."

"We're heading home?"

"I believe so, for a little while at least." Grinning, she held onto him tight. "It appears we've a busy time ahead of us in ensuring our future fae-shifter Matheson line no longer nears extinction."

"This is what I now live for, to see each mated pair of fae blood join together as one. Your duty is my duty."

"Then we need to leave and continue that duty now." She swirled the air and opened a portal. The wind tunneled around them and they fell away into the dark abyss, both holding onto each other as they crossed the heavenly realm through time.

Love knew no bounds, could cross the centuries.

And now, 'twas time for another great adventure to unfold.

Author's Note

In the twelfth century, clan Matheson settled around the area of Loch Alsh, Loch Carron, and Kintail, and gave their allegiance to clan MacDonald whose chiefs were the Lords of the Isles. Clan Matheson became a large and powerful clan with a force of around two-thousand men, although by the middle of the sixteenth century they'd diminished greatly in size and influence due to the blood feuds raging across the isles at that time. This warring left them to possess less than a third of their original Matheson property on Loch Alsh.

It's also well known in history that clan Matheson also forged an alliance with clan MacKenzie during the middle ages, which meant at times the two clans fought side by side, yet also against each other when clan Matheson found themselves stuck in the middle of the feuding between the MacDonalds and the MacKenzies. Clan MacRae also aligned themselves strongly with clan MacKenzie, their allied relationship including many intermarriages between them. Within this series my hope has been to capture the difficulties faced between all these great clans, and all while spinning stories in my own unique way.

Certainly across all the books I've written involving the three primary clans of Matheson, MacKenzie, and MacDonald,

I've tried my best to show how their feuding and alliances made, moved back and forth throughout the years. I dearly love all these clans, can understand their struggles and losses, their conquests and wins, as well as how they attempted to remain as honorable as they could throughout it all.

This story is woven with as much accuracy to the period and locations as possible, although any mistakes made are mine alone. Please feel free to search for any of my other works. I simply adore strong heroines, and have a ton of fun matching them with their honorable alpha heroes.

**Also available in paperback
Scottish Historical Romance**

Traveling through time…for a Highlander.

Highlander Heat Series

Highlander's Castle, Book One

Highlander's Magic, Book Two

Highlander's Charm, Book Three

Highlander's Guardian, Book Four

Highlander's Faerie, Book Five

Highlander's Champion, Book Six

by Joanne Wadsworth

Looking for more sexy Scottish adventure?

Catch a teaser excerpt of the next book in this series.

Highlander's Shifter

The Matheson Brothers, Book Ten

by Joanne Wadsworth

Highlander's Shifter

The Matheson Brothers, Book Ten

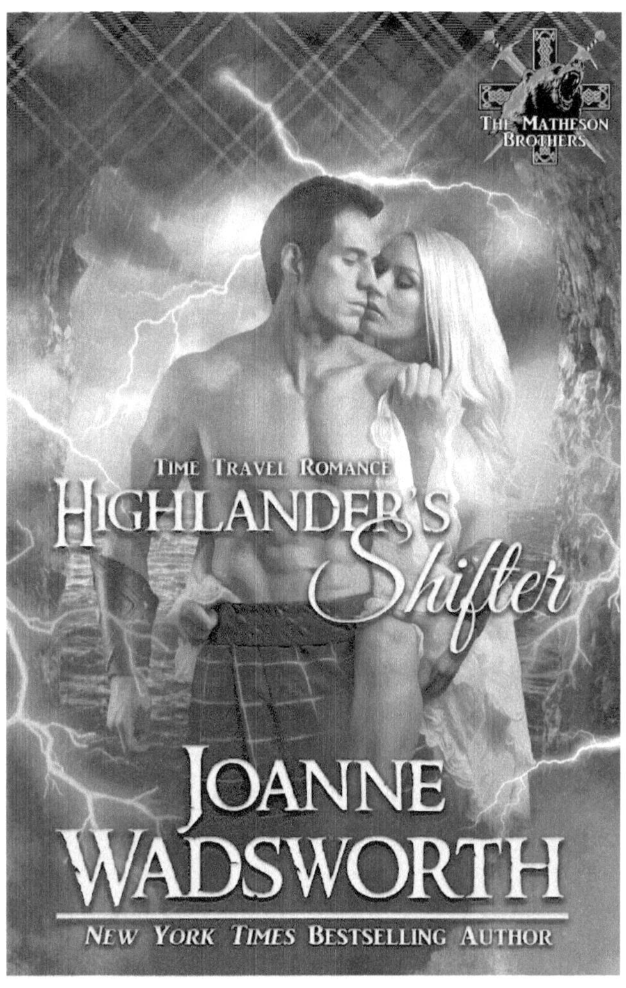

Teaser Excerpt

Jamie slid one arm around Bella's waist and tipped her back against the warm black metal of his SUV door before muttering, "This is a dangerous mission, with not only two rogue bears on the loose but me as well, and I'm one damn hungry unmated male after a bond. Don't take my warning lightly, Annabella."

"Bella. And I'm well aware you're one damn hungry male." She ran her hands up over his large biceps and curled her fingers around them. "Clearly you need to stake your claim while we're here. I understand why with two possible rogues so near, so whatever you need to do to calm your bear, then do it. Stake whatever claim you wish. Cover me in your scent, and if that's not enough, I give you permission to kiss me."

"I want to do more than saturate you in my scent." He nuzzled her neck, scraped his teeth back and forth across her pounding pulse point and sent all her thoughts scattering as he did. "I'm ravenous, have been walking an incredibly tight line around you of late."

"And I trust you to keep walking along that tight line and not to deviate from it." Certainly no man had ever made her feel so safe and secure as Jamie did, no matter the current frustration rising within him and leaking past his guards. "I wouldn't mind if you took me up on my offer though. Smother me in your scent and kiss me."

She'd been dreaming of how he'd kiss her, how he'd touch his lips to hers and share the same breath as her. His gaze narrowed and that delicious rumble vibrated again in his chest and rose upward. It left his throat in a snarly rasp and she couldn't help but tighten her grip on his arms. "I dare you to kiss me, Jamie."

"Careful, Bella. You're treading into dangerous territory."

"And you're not treading into it quite fast enough."

The Matheson Brothers Continued

Highlander's Kiss, Book Four
Highlander's Heart, Book Five
Highlander's Sword, Book Six

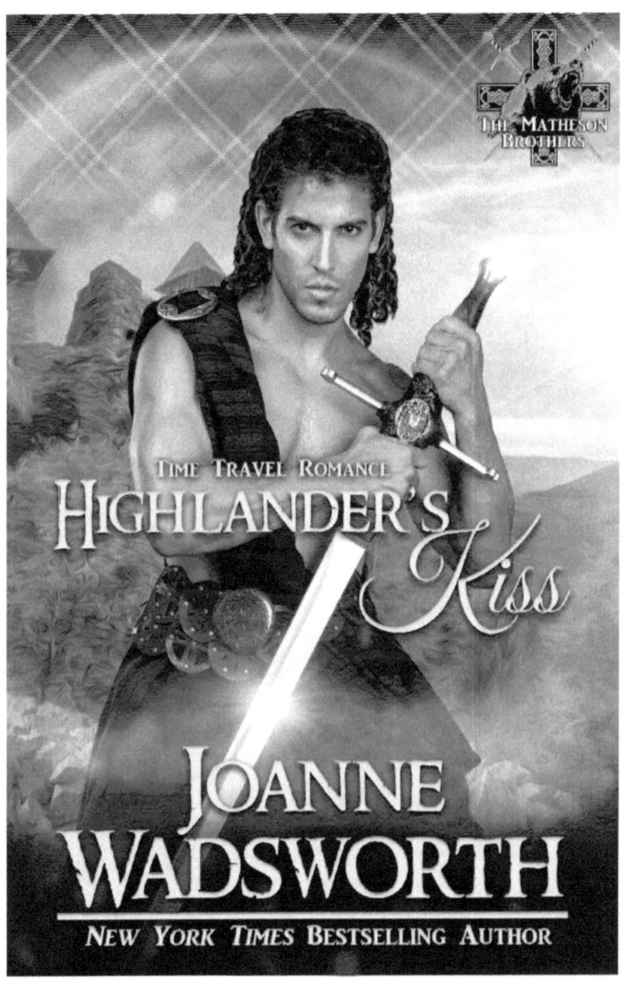

JOANNE WADSWORTH

The Matheson Brothers Continued

The Matheson Brothers Continued

Highlander's Shifter, Book Ten
Highlander's Claim, Book Eleven
Highlander's Courage, Book Twelve
Highlander's Mermaid, Book Thirteen

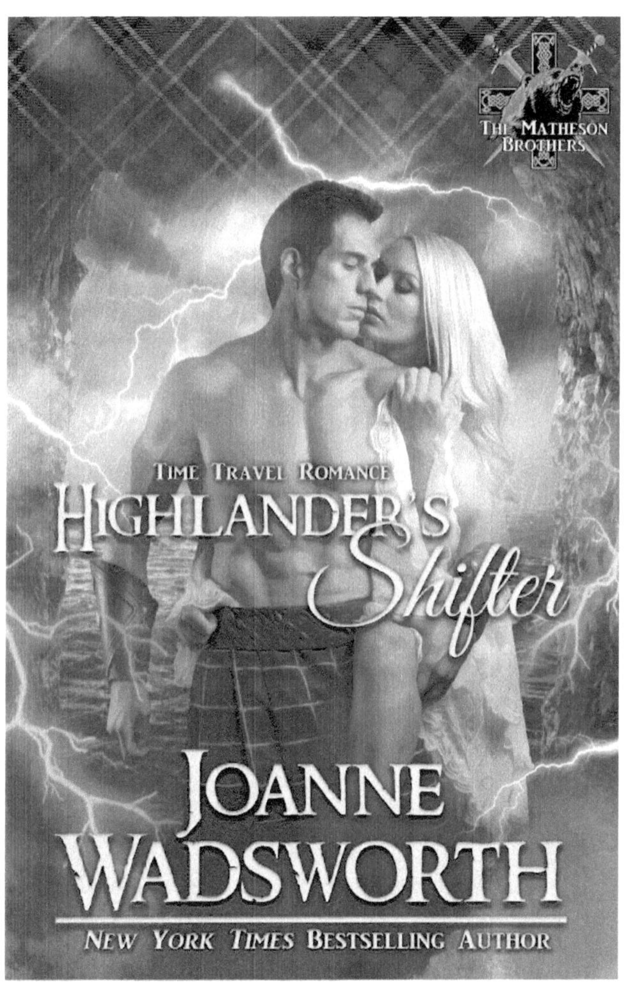

JOANNE WADSWORTH

Highlander Heat

Regency Brides

The Duke's Bride, Book One
The Earl's Bride, Book Two
The Wartime Bride, Book Three
The Earl's Secret Bride, Book Four
The Prince's Bride, Book Five
Her Pirate Prince, Book Six

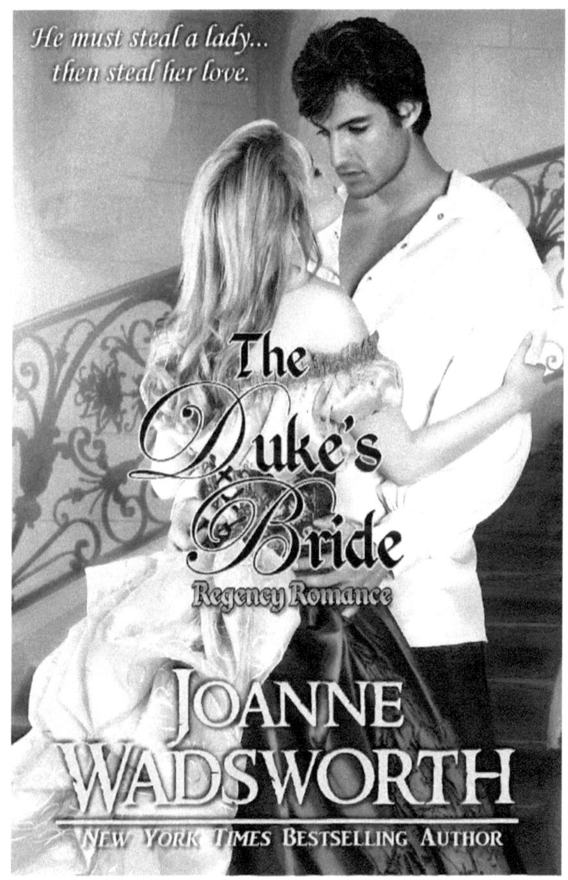

Billionaire Bodyguards

Billionaire Bodyguard Attraction, Book One
Billionaire Bodyguard Boss, Book Two
Billionaire Bodyguard Fling, Book Three

JOANNE WADSWORTH

Joanne Wadsworth is a *New York Times* and *USA Today* Bestselling Author who adores getting lost in the world of romance, no matter what era in time that might be. Hot alpha Highlanders hound her, demanding their stories are told and she's devoted to ensuring they meet their match, whether that be with a feisty lass from the present or far in the past.

Living on a tiny island at the bottom of the world, she calls New Zealand home. Big-dreamer, hoarder of chocolate, and addicted to juicy watermelons since the age of five, she chases after her four energetic children and has her own hunky hubby on the side.

So come and join in all the fun, because this kiwi girl promises to give you her "Hot-Highlander" oath, to bring you a heart-pounding, sexy adventure from the moment you turn the first page. This is where romance meets fantasy and adventure…

To learn more about Joanne and her works, visit
http://www.joannewadsworth.com